"Let's get you home."

Chap wrapped an arm around Hailey.

She clamped a hand over a yawn. "I won't argue with you."

The drive back to the ranch was uneventful. She relaxed enough to close her eyes, but they popped open when she felt the truck swerve sharply.

She watched Chap tap the brakes, but nothing happened. Another tap. Harder this time. No joy.

He applied the parking brake to no avail.

"Chap—" Her voice quivered in the dark cab.

The narrow road, flanked by a canyon wall on one side and a cliff on the other, left no margin for error. Turning too far in one direction would ram them against the unforgiving granite face of the canyon. Too far in the other would take them over the edge of the mountainside.

Patches of black ice had already made navigating the road dicey. Without brakes, it was deadly.

"Hold on," he said. He didn't have to tell her twice.

The truck was careening down the road with no brakes.

Jane M. Choate dreamed of writing from the time she was a small child when she entertained friends with outlandish stories complete with happily-ever-after endings. Writing for Love Inspired Suspense is a dream come true. Jane is the proud mother of five children, grandmother to ten grandchildren and staff to one cat who believes she is of royal descent.

Books by Jane M. Choate

Love Inspired Suspense

Keeping Watch
The Littlest Witness
Shattered Secrets
High-Risk Investigation
Inherited Threat
Stolen Child
Secrets from the Past
Lethal Corruption
Rocky Mountain Vendetta
Christmas Witness Survival

Visit the Author Profile page at LoveInspired.com.

CHRISTMAS WITNESS SURVIVAL

JANE M. CHOATE

LOVE INSPIRED SUSPENSE
INSPIRATIONAL ROMANCE

LOVE INSPIRED® SUSPENSE
INSPIRATIONAL ROMANCE

Recycling programs
for this product may
not exist in your area.

ISBN-13: 978-1-335-59922-3

Christmas Witness Survival

Love Inspired
22 Adelaide St. West, 41st Floor
Toronto, Ontario M5H 4E3, Canada
www.LoveInspired.com

Printed in U.S.A.

Blessed is the man that endureth temptation:
for when he is tried, he shall receive the crown of life,
which the Lord hath promised to them that love him.
—*James* 1:12

One of the best things about being a writer is getting to do research and learn about things completely out of my wheelhouse. For this book, I researched Navy SEALs and learned that they are often referred to as door-kickers. What a great name for the courageous men who protect our nation at the risk of their own lives. This book is dedicated to the door-kickers and their families.

ONE

Though the temperature was well below freezing, Hailey Davenport escaped to the second-floor balcony for a few minutes to avoid the noise and confusion of the Christmas Eve party. Since the party was being held to celebrate her engagement to Douglas Lawson as much as to herald Christmas, she shouldn't have left, but she desperately needed a moment of quiet to gather her thoughts. She was more accustomed to being behind the scenes at parties as a caterer than being front and center stage.

Laughter, the twinkle of fairy lights and the glitter of jewels adorning designer gowns made a fitting backdrop for what was being hailed as the society event of the year. Well-known in the Colorado social scene, Douglas Lawson was news in every media outlet, and his engagement was greeted with the same acclaim as though he'd been royalty. More than once, Hailey had heard the engagement described as that of one between the prince and the cook.

When goose bumps prickled her skin, she turned to go back inside, but angry voices from below snagged her attention.

She swiveled and stared.

Doug grabbed a man's collar, nearly lifting him off the ground. She'd rarely seen her fiancé angry, certainly not enough to do physical harm to another, but the coldness in his eyes was enough to have her draw back.

The other man was one she'd seen around the glass-and-wood mansion that was Doug's house in the foothills northwest of Fort Collins, Colorado. She'd assumed he was one of the many people who worked to keep the operation of Doug's dozens of enterprises running smoothly.

She didn't know what all his businesses entailed, but she knew that he was a major player in Colorado's corporate community. That he'd paid attention to her, a small-time caterer, was still a mystery.

Listening to other people's conversations was never a good idea, she told herself and, not wanting to eavesdrop, she began to turn away, but the intensity of the words pulled her back.

"You thought stealing from me—me!— was a good idea?" Despite his anger, Doug's words were so carefully articulated that each one seemed to make a statement on its own.

Even though the words weren't directed at her, she shrank from them. Doug never demeaned himself by shouting; instead, his voice went deadly quiet. With a wince, she recalled when she'd accidentally seated two business rivals next to each other at a party she'd planned for him. At the end of the evening, he'd told her, in an excruciatingly soft voice, that she was never to make such a mistake again.

She never did.

"Please, boss. You know I'm good for the money. I'll pay you back. With interest."

"Oh, so now you remember I'm the boss?" Doug's voice held a silky quality that made her shiver over and beyond that of the frigid temperature.

"We've been together for a long time," the other man said, voice nearing a sob.

"And that's supposed to excuse you from stealing from me?" The question was said in that same smooth tone that was somehow more frightening than an enraged one.

"N-no. That's not what I meant." The man gave a smile, though it looked sickly. "Only that you and me are buddies. Been buddies for five years now. That's gotta be worth something."

"What did you mean, Mikey?"

"I just meant that you know I'm good for it."

"How much do you think your friendship is worth? Fifty thousand dollars? A hundred thousand?"

"No. But I only took twenty-five."

"Oh, so you think your friendship is worth twenty-five grand to me?" Doug's tone was quizzical.

"Like I said, I'll pay you back. With interest."

"I think I'll take payment now. With interest." Doug pulled a gun from the waist of his designer tuxedo. And fired.

Though the shot wasn't overly loud—did the gun have a silencer?—it made a crack in the murmur of the Christmas music playing in the background.

The man named Mikey clutched his chest, a confused expression on his face, as though he didn't understand what had happened, then crumpled to the ground.

No.

She clapped a hand over her mouth to keep from screaming. Surely, she hadn't seen what her eyes told her she had witnessed. She was imagining things. The cold. That was it. It was playing tricks with her eyes, with her mind.

But no. She looked again, saw Doug standing over the man she'd thought was his friend. He gestured to the two men who had been standing in the shadows. "You know what to do."

"You got it, boss," one said.

They picked up the body and made to carry it away.

Hailey started to back out of the balcony, but she bumped into a patio table and knocked over a drink someone had left there.

The shattering of crystal had three sets of eyes lifting in her direction.

"Hailey, let me explain," Doug called from below. "It's not what you think. Please, honey, I can fix this."

Sick terror bloomed inside her. She didn't want or need explanations. There was only one thing she could do, and she did it.

She fled.

"Leave him and get her," she heard Doug order the men. On the tail of that came another order for two more men to get rid of the body.

Fortunately, she knew the house well enough to remember there was a back staircase leading to the kitchen. She ran down the stairs and out the kitchen door. Cold seared her lungs.

Think.

The men Doug sent after her would believe she'd try to get off the estate, but that was a fool's move. The estate stretched for miles. There was no way she could make it that far, not dressed as she was and in the icy weather.

No. She had to find a place to hide. She thought of the massive parking garage that held sixteen vehicles. If she hid out in one, she'd have time to consider her next move. Somehow, she had to get to town and then go to the police.

She crept to the garage and found the side door unlocked. Not willing to turn on a light and risk giving away her location, she picked her way through the darkness. She found a car unlocked and slipped into the back.

A black wool coat lay on the seat and she used it to cover herself. It was then that she noticed it was Doug's coat. How could she have chosen his vehicle in which to hide? In the dark, she hadn't been able to tell whose car it was.

Voices alerted her that she wasn't alone. Two men climbed into the front seat. Her pulse went into overdrive when she recognized Doug's voice.

Did he know she was there and was baiting her to reveal herself?

"How did the woman get away?" he asked, disgust ripe in his voice.

"We searched everywhere, boss." She recognized the voice of Doug's second-hand man.

"We've got to find her. In the meantime, I want to see the police chief. If she makes her way to town, I wouldn't put it past a Goody Two-shoes like her to go straight to the police with what she saw."

"The chief's on the payroll. He knows what side his bread is buttered on."

There was no way she could go to the police now, not when she knew Doug owned the police chief.

The trip to town was torturously slow. Any minute, she expected Doug to lean over the seat and expose her.

When the car stopped, she held her breath. What if the other man stayed in the car?

"I want you with me," Doug said to his employee.

"Sure thing, boss."

Both men exited the car. She peered above the seat, saw that they were walking into the police station. As quickly as possible, given her long evening dress, Hailey slipped from the car, taking Doug's coat with her. Though she loathed using anything of his, she needed it. In the pockets, she found a pair of thick black gloves and a watch cap which she quickly pulled on. Though they were far too large, they provided protection against the cold.

Could she hitch a ride out of town to one of the truck stops along the highway? Maybe then she could find her way out of Colorado on one of the big rigs that made its way across the state every day.

Hitchhiking wasn't a smart move, but with no family or friends to call on, she didn't have a choice. So anxious had she been to escape Doug's house that she'd left without a purse and didn't have even a few dollars with her.

She made her way to the side of the road. It was so cold that she imagined she could feel her lips turning blue. Resolutely, she stuck out her thumb and prayed.

When a nice-looking, middle-aged couple stopped and asked her if she needed help, she almost cried. "Y-yes," she stuttered.

"We can't take you far," the lady said, "but we can get you to the highway, if that would help."

"That would be gr-great." Her teeth were chattering so badly that she could barely get out the words. "Thank you."

"Get in, miss," the man said. "You look cold enough to give penguins a run for their money."

"I am that." She climbed into the back seat and prayed the couple wouldn't have questions for her.

If they did, they were tactful enough to keep them to themselves, but that didn't keep the woman from darting concerned looks in Hailey's direction. They took her as far as a large truck stop.

"You be careful," the woman said. "This isn't any place for a lady. Are you sure we can't take you somewhere else?"

"No, thank you, ma'am. I'll be fine." The lie stuck in Hailey's throat, but there was no way she could involve this sweet couple in her problems.

The lady handed her two twenties. "You look like you could use this."

Hailey wanted to turn down the offer, but practicality took over. "I can't thank you enough. If you give me your address, I'll repay you. I promise."

"Return the favor to someone else someday," the woman said. "That's payment enough."

Blinking back tears, Hailey thanked them again and tucked the twenties into a coat pocket.

Her circumstances couldn't have been more grim, but the Lord had cast His mercy upon her in the form of these kind people who had appeared just when she'd needed them. She had never doubted His love. He would see her through this just as He had everything else, including living on the streets when she was barely eighteen.

For as long as she could remember, she'd longed for someone to love her and to love in return, someone with whom she could make a family. She thought she'd found that with Doug. Instead, she'd found a cheap imitation of the real thing, one that had quickly tarnished and shown its true self.

She huddled deeper into the too-big coat and made her way through the slush and ice.

When she saw a pickup truck with a Wyoming license plate, she picked the lock—a skill she'd learned on the streets—and climbed inside. "Lord, I need Your help. I know You won't let me down."

Michael "Chap" Chapman cradled the hot drink between his hands and wondered what had possessed him to make a trip to his ranch in Wyoming on the coldest day of the year. Driving usually calmed him, but not so tonight. Nor had working out in S&J's gym or shooting on the practice range.

He had been driving for a couple of hours and decided he could use a break at the truck stop for coffee and a short rest. Driving while tired was a recipe for disaster.

Then, again, nothing had felt right since his fiancée, Lori, had been murdered almost two years ago. The holidays were an especially hard time; he'd gotten through one Christmas without her already and had grappled with the heartbreak of losing her. He'd thought, hoped, that catching her killer would have eased the pain, and, in a way it had, but he still struggled at this time of year, a reminder of all that he'd lost.

As soon as her name appeared in his mind, the breath left his body, like air being sucked away in a dust storm. Anguish built inside him until he grew tired of fighting it and let the memories have their way.

He'd asked Lori to marry him just a week before she'd died. Neither of them could have known that an ex-con, someone Chap had put away during his years as a US marshal, would come gunning for him. When he'd stooped to tie his shoe, the gunman's bullet had hit Lori, killing her instantly.

He'd tracked down the shooter and had come within a hairbreadth of killing him before his better self had taken over. After turning the man in to the police, he had walked away. Not a day went by that he didn't wish the bullet had found its target, taking his life instead of Lori's.

For the first six months following her death, he hadn't left the ranch. He'd turned everything over to his foreman and holed up in his room, even taking his meals there, as he'd struggled to find a reason to keep living. He'd taken a leave of absence from S&J and cut off all contact with his friends.

Decay was a pervasive disease.

When he'd finally joined the land of the living again, his friends had been shocked to see the change in him, his face haggard, his once-muscular body so thin as to look emaciated.

It had been then that he'd known he needed to do something. He'd started eating right, working out and, when he felt ready, asked for his job back at S&J Security/Protection in Denver.

These days, he pushed himself hard, dividing his time between his ranch in eastern Wyoming and his job with S&J. There was no downtime for him; he feared if he stopped working, even for a minute, the grief would catch him unawares. Just thinking about Lori's murder felt like a large stone crushing his chest until he had to gasp for breath. Her death had shifted his relationship with the Lord, ripping apart the faith that had once been his and leaving bitterness in its place.

The temperature hovered around five degrees. He must be getting old as the cold permeated his bones and sent a dull throb through his joints. It didn't help that a couple of old bullet wounds exacerbated the aches and pains when the temperature reached a certain point. He pulled his black Stetson low over his ears.

Pickups, SUVs and huge semis filled the parking lot. It looked like half of Colorado had gathered there to get out of the cold. The smell of diesel and fried food filled the air, the signature scent of truck stops everywhere.

Garish red and green lights, meant to be festive, he supposed, framed a large window, blinking on and off. They only added to his sour mood. He hadn't celebrated Christmas last year, the first since Lori had been killed, and he didn't expect to celebrate tomorrow either.

The snow had stopped, leaving ice in its wake, which had turned the roads treacherous. Fortunately, his pickup had a heavy-duty suspension and chains on its tires.

He wasn't worried about making it the next seventy-five miles. He'd grown up in the area, as accustomed to the biting cold of a Colorado winter as he was to the frequently brutal heat of summer.

No, he had other things on his mind. Or, he amended silently, in his heart.

Enough.

After taking a pit stop for both him and Sam, he and the German shepherd made their way back to his truck. Sam didn't mind the cold and trotted through puddles and snow with gleeful enthusiasm.

"Nothing slows you down, does it, boy?" Chap asked with a pat to the dog's large head.

Sam woofed his pleasure. When they reached the truck, however, he gave a low growl that had Chap tensing. As the dog's hackles raised, Chap knew something was up.

His reached for the .38 that was strapped to his hip and opened the door to the crew seat.

A startled cry greeted him.

He found an arm and yanked out whoever was in there with a hard jerk. "Who are you? And what are you doing in my truck?"

He got a better look at the intruder and saw that it was a woman. She couldn't have been any more than five-one or five-two and no more than a hundred and five pounds. Blond hair, green eyes, and a small dimple at the corner of her mouth gave her face an elfin air, but it was the fear that tightened her pretty features that gave him pause.

He relaxed his grip. "Want to tell me how you got in there?"

"I picked the lock."

"*You* picked the lock?" There was more to this woman than he'd first thought. "Where'd you learn to do that?"

She tilted her chin. "On the streets."

Okay. Interesting. But he wasn't about to be tricked into letting a stranger in his truck, no matter how pretty she was.

"I'm guessing you want a ride."

"I have to get out of here." Desperation punched every syllable.

Frozen tears speckled her face, making her appear impossibly young and vulnerable, and he did his best to resist the protective instincts that threatened to flare up. "I got that. The question is why."

"My...uh...husband threatened to kill me. I'm afraid he'll find me if I stay here. He's gets mean when he's angry."

Her fear was real, but something about her story didn't ring true for him. Aside from that, the last thing Chap wanted was to get involved in a quarrel between a husband and wife, but he kept his thoughts to himself.

"Why choose my rig?" he asked.

"I saw the Wyoming tags and guessed you were heading out of state. Wanted to get as far away as possible."

Her hands were encased in men's gloves, so he couldn't see if she wore a ring or not. He put that away to consider later. She pulled off her left glove and pushed wet strands of hair from her face.

It was then that he noticed she wore a showy engagement ring with a diamond the size of a man's knuckle, but no wedding band. That kind of engagement ring came with an equally ostentatious wedding band. Didn't it?

Her gaze collided with his. A flush moved up her neck to settle on her face. It wasn't hard to figure that she knew he'd been staring at the ring. She twisted it around, probably to hide the diamond, but the big stone wouldn't allow her to close her fingers over it.

His gaze drifted back to her face. She looked scared, he thought again. Scratch scared. Make that terrified.

He understood fear, having experienced his fair share of it while deployed in Afghanistan—the Stand in military parlance—and then again while working as a US marshal and as an operative for S&J Security/Protection. Fear was part and parcel of being human. The only way Chap knew to control it was to keep moving forward. Retreating, even for a moment, was to invite the fear to take root.

Knowing that the enemy had you in the crosshairs of an automatic weapon tended to make fear up close and personal. Being highly trained didn't banish fear; on the contrary, it made it all the more real.

No, he didn't fault the lady for being scared, but he was pretty sure she'd lied to him about why she was on the run. His suspicion was backed up when he asked for her name.

"What's your name?"

"Ha… Hazel. Hazel…" A longer pause. "Da… Danvers."

That was most likely another lie, along with the story about a husband threatening to kill her, but he didn't call her on it.

Yet.

"Will you help me?" Fresh tears gathered in her eyes, and he knew he was lost.

The truck stop was known for its rough clientele, the police routinely called in to break up fights. And worse. A murder had recently taken place in the parking lot when rival gangs had argued over turf. Drug dealing wasn't uncommon, along with prostitution and muggings. She wouldn't last five minutes inside, less in the parking lot where predators tended to lurk whatever the weather.

"Okay. I'll give you a ride. Just till we get to the border." The gruff words caused a wave of shame to wash through him. Two years ago, he would have offered help willingly, but a lot can happen in a year, and the shame was now colored with grief.

"Thank you."

The quaver in her voice told him more than words could just how frightened she was. He couldn't let her fend on her own. It wasn't in him. Ice pellets spit from the sky, stinging his face. Automatically, he hunched over her in an attempt to protect her.

She had to be freezing, even with a man's coat draped over her. And what was that she was wearing? Though he could see only the bottom few inches of the dress beneath the overlarge coat, it looked like an evening gown.

But that made no sense. A woman didn't flee an abusive situation wearing an evening dress.

Curiouser and curiouser.

No matter the circumstances, he wasn't about to take a stranger with him until he'd made certain she wasn't armed.

"Turn your pockets inside out."

She did as he ordered and turned out her pockets. Nothing.

He hadn't expected anything, but he'd had to be sure.

"I don't have a weapon, if that's what you're thinking."

He believed her, but it was reckless to invite anyone into the truck without checking him or her out.

"Take off your hat."

She wore a man's black watch cap, probably from the same man whose coat she wore. It was Safety 101. Make certain you could see a suspect's eyes and facial expression. That meant no hats or scarves. Not that the lady was a suspect, but better to practice caution than to be caught unaware.

She pulled the cap from her head, then shook out her hair. "Satisfied?"

"That'll do," he said gruffly, feeling like a heel.

Her teeth chattered again, reminding him that he needed to get her out of the unrelenting wind. "C'mon," he said. There was that gruffness again. "Let's get you warm. You look cold enough to shatter into pieces any moment now."

The grateful look she cast him sent another wave of shame through him. "Thank you," she said again, worsening the shame.

"No problem."

There was more going on here than she was telling him, and though he didn't like being lied to, he had to help her. His conscience wouldn't allow him to do anything else.

So much for a quiet trip to his ranch in Wyoming. He had a feeling things were going to get interesting before he and the lady reached the border.

Hailey had told the pickup's owner the truth when she said she'd chosen his truck because it bore Wyoming tags, but she'd lied about everything else. Lies didn't go down easy with her, and she wanted to snatch them back, to come clean with him.

Shame trickled through her as she acknowledged that she'd not only lied to him, she had compounded the lie by continuing it.

That wasn't like her. The only excuse she could offer was that she'd been—still was, for that matter—terrified.

Over his shoulder, she saw two men working their way down the row of pickup trucks and semis. Though she couldn't know if they were working for Doug, it made sense that his goons would be checking truck stops. Fortunately, they had their backs turned to her, talking to a trucker.

"Please, I don't want those men to see me." She pointed to the two men who were growing closer and closer.

The cowboy gave a slight turn then, before she knew what was happening, picked her up and lifted her inside the truck cab.

"Get down." He took a blanket from the back seat of the crew cab and draped it over her. "Sam, get up here."

The dog jumped over the seat and settled on the passenger side, his big tail covering her. He was so close, Hailey could smell the kibble on his breath.

She did the only thing she could. She prayed.

A rap at the window sent her heartbeat into overtime.

The cowboy lowered his window. "What's up?"

"We're looking for a woman. Small, blonde. Probably in evening clothes."

"How come you're looking for her?"

A long pause. She imagined the men looking at each other, trying to come up with a plausible explanation. "She's our boss's little sister," one said at last. "She and her brother had a fight. She ran away but didn't take her diabetes medication with her. We just want to make sure she's all right. Our boss is really protective of her and pretty worried right now."

Pinpricks of fear washed over her scalp as she waited for the cowboy's answer. She'd known he hadn't believed her answers to his questions. Would he turn her over to these men, men she knew planned on killing her?

"Got it," he said. "But there's no woman here. Only me and Sam."

Sam growled.

She pictured the men backing away at the menacing sound and held her breath. Did they buy it?

"Okay. Thanks."

The cowboy raised the window. "It's clear," he said after several minutes had passed.

Cautiously, she inched her way up. The men were gone, but she was faced with another problem. Did he believe her? Or did he believe the men who had managed to sound so convincing?

"You don't have to worry," he said. "I didn't believe them."

"Why not?"

"They were more interested in giving your description than in being concerned over your supposed diabetes. By the way, you don't have diabetes, do you?"

"No." She drew a shaky breath. "And thank you."

"You don't have to thank me. Just stay down until we're out of the parking lot."

She had no problem doing just that.

When she finally climbed into the seat again

and pulled her seat belt around her Sam having given it up with a plaintive woof that sounded a lot like a huff of annoyance, she took her first normal breath in hours. Her chest hurt; the result, she supposed, of the extreme cold.

How could the man she thought she loved have turned into a stranger, one who had killed another man without hesitation and was most likely looking to kill her as well? She didn't know this new Doug. What's more, she didn't want to know him.

Could he have changed so much in the seven months she'd known him?

Common sense told her that he probably hadn't changed at all, that she was only now seeing the true man. The man she'd fallen in love with didn't exist, had never existed.

Having spent the last eight years on her own, some of those living on the street until she could find a job and afford a place to live, she'd known rough conditions, rough people, but never had she faced anything like this. And never would she have suspected that Douglas Lawson, prominent in the Denver social scene, was a stone-cold killer. With his polished manners and exquisite tastes, he was the epitome of a gentleman.

Or so she'd thought.

Inside the truck, as she began to warm up, she

got her first real look at the man without pellets of snow obstructing her vision. In the light of the dash, she saw the integrity in his gaze, that and kindness. Right now, she needed both.

He was clean-shaven, his face composed of angles and planes that gave him a hard look until you looked at his eyes. They softened his expression in ways he probably wasn't aware of.

"Thank you," she said.

"You already said that."

"Oh. I'm sorry. I mean… I don't know what I mean." The hated tears threatened to spill over.

"It's okay. Let's get on our way." His voice gentled. "Mind telling me what you're doing in an evening gown?"

She looked down to see the hem of her dress peeking out from under the coat she'd taken. "It's a long story."

"I've got time."

How much did she tell him? Douglas Lawson had a long reach. Even though the cowboy appeared to be honest and forthright, could she trust him with the truth?

She studied his face and saw strength there, but something more as well. Pain etched the lines fanning from his eyes, as though they had seen too much of the world's ugliness and were struggling to contain overwhelming grief.

There she went again. Making things up. More than one foster parent had told her that she was too fanciful. *Plant your feet on the ground before those notions of yours get you in trouble,* one foster mother had said when the young Hailey had made up a story about a unicorn princess and a prince fashioned after mythology's Pegasus.

What was wrong with having notions? she had wondered, but she'd refrained from spinning more stories for her foster brothers and sisters, much to their disappointment.

She needed the cowboy's help and couldn't afford to antagonize him by asking what had hurt him so badly.

"I don't know your name," she said.

"Michael Chapman. My friends call me Chap."

She liked the sound of the name. It suited him. Hailey knew she was being vetted now. He asked questions. She answered. When she stumbled over some of the answers, she knew she'd lost points with him. Should she just tell him the truth and take the consequences?

What if he didn't believe her? Would he stop the truck and order her to get out? The truth was so outlandish that she wouldn't have believed it if she hadn't lived through it.

She trembled as she recalled the passionless

way Doug had killed another man. It had been done with such coldness that she wondered what she'd ever seen in him, much less how she'd thought herself in love with him.

Doug must have been a consummate actor to have fooled her so completely. Or she had been a naïve fool to have believed he loved her. Maybe both.

All of this swirled through her mind as the cowboy subjected her to a thorough study.

"Have you made up your mind?" she asked.

"About what?"

"About me."

He glanced at her then turned his attention back to the road. "I don't know. I'll let you know when I do."

That was fair.

She didn't doubt that when he gave his word, he kept it.

He slid another glance her way. From the expression in his eyes, he knew she was lying, but he hadn't called her on it. Yet.

She dipped her head, unwilling to let him see her eyes.

"Most folks lie when they're scared," he said.

Should she tell him? How did she know she could trust him?

"Sounds like you've had some experience with people lying to you," she said.

"Some." He left it at that, leaving her to wonder what kind of experiences he was referring to.

Right now, she needed his help. If not for him... She didn't allow her thoughts to go beyond that. The images in her mind were sufficient to leave her frightened to the very core.

Just as she thought they were in the clear, something hit them from behind. The force propelled her forward, only the seat belt prevented her from crashing into the dashboard.

Chap turned to her, his expression as hard as his voice. "Those two yahoos are behind us."

"What are we going to do?" She worked to keep her voice steady, free of the nerves that had settled in her belly. He didn't need to know that she was fresh out of courage.

"Hang on. Things are going to get dicey."

She hung on. And prayed.

TWO

Chap watched from his mirror as the SUV rammed them again. His mouth tightened as he punched the accelerator.

The men after them were in for a surprise.

Though his pickup appeared to be old and battered, he had installed extra safety measures such as bullet-proof glass, along with a high-performance engine. He gunned the engine now. The truck shot forward, leaving the SUV far behind.

He had to exit the highway. If he could get far enough ahead of the men chasing them, he could turn off the main thoroughfare and choose any one of a half dozen roads that would take them to the state line.

He didn't let up on the gas until he'd left the SUV in his rearview mirror. *Good.*

What had given them away?

"It's my fault," the lady said, her voice so low that he had to strain to catch the words.

"What do you mean?"

"This." She pointed to the passenger's side door.

He leaned over and saw it. The hem of her dress was caught in the door. The men must have seen the fabric as they'd walked away. They'd only been biding their time, waiting to attack once Chap and Hazel, or whatever her name was, were on the road and away from possible help.

"I'd say that was my fault. I was the one who closed the door."

"And I should have been more careful to pull my dress all the way in."

"We could play the blame game all night. It doesn't matter. The men know you're with me. That's the only thing that matters right now."

"I'm sorry. I shouldn't have gotten you involved."

He couldn't let her carry that kind of guilt. "Hey, if I hadn't wanted to help, I wouldn't have given you a ride. And I can take care of myself."

A small smile leaked out. "Thanks for that." The smile disappeared. "What are we going to do?"

"Find a different road."

She drew a visible breath at his long hesitation. "If you want to let me out, I understand."

There was a tremor in her voice, but she held his gaze, letting him know that she meant every word. The lady not only had guts but also integrity. The words hadn't come easily, he knew. He saw the struggle on her face as she mined for inner strength.

That did it. "You think I'd throw you out in this weather with a couple of your husband's goons chasing you?"

"No. But I needed to say it. No one would blame you for letting me out and washing your hands of the whole thing."

"I'll take you to the border."

"Then what?"

He didn't know. "We'll sort that out when we get there."

There was little traffic, which made spotting tails easier. Only a burly SUV occupied the stretch of road they were currently on. When it made a wide U-turn, reversing direction, and barreled straight for them, Chap wasn't surprised. He'd expected another try. He just hadn't expected it this soon.

He didn't steer around the SUV. Nor did his hands tighten on the steering wheel. They retained a firm grip, but that was all.

"It's coming right at us," the woman said when collision seemed inevitable.

"I know. I guess we're going to see who wins at playing chicken."

At the last moment, the SUV veered and landed in the deep ravine parallel to the road. He allowed a small smile to play at his lips at the driver's probable chagrin.

He heard her breath catch then release.

"How did you know they'd give in?" she asked.

"I figured them to be bullies. Bullies generally tend to turn tail and run if you call their bluff."

"You've had experience with them."

"I've met my fair share. In Afghanistan. Here. To a one, they're cowards. They pick on those they think are weaker and then are surprised when their target stands up and fights back."

The men chasing the woman at his side didn't know it, but they'd just ensured that he would stick by her, whatever came. He didn't know what her story was, but she'd just gained an ally.

"I could have used that advice when I was in grade school and the other kids made fun of me."

"Why? Why make fun of you?" Even with her hair wet, her makeup smudged, and in the too-big coat that swallowed her like a whale slurping up a guppy, she was gorgeous, and he assumed the child she'd been had been adorable.

"I was a foster kid. I bounced around between different homes. Some were good. Some not so much." She lifted her shoulders in a small shrug.

"I'm sorry."

"Don't be. I learned what I needed for when I was on my own." In the muted light cast by the dashboard, he saw a flush stain her cheeks. "Not everything but enough to get by." In the time that one heartbeat moved to the next, she said, "I know you don't want to hear more thanks, but I have to say it. You risked your life for me. Not many people would do that."

"Maybe you don't know the right people."

"Maybe you're right."

They didn't talk much after that.

Chap wrestled with what to do next. He knew he couldn't leave her at the border, not with two hoods chasing her. He also knew she was lying to him. Ordinarily, that would have been a deal-breaker and he'd have kicked her out, but he sensed there was more to her story.

One thing he didn't doubt was that she was in trouble and scared out of her wits.

Hailey clenched her jaw in an attempt to keep the fear at bay. The last thing she wanted was to let the cowboy know how truly terrified she was that he'd change his mind and tell her to get out.

When she felt Chap's gaze on her, she gave him what she thought of as her don't-mess-with-me-if-you-want-to-live look. It had saved her life more than once when she'd been on her own.

"Relax," he said, apparently reading her thoughts. "I'm not going to kick you out."

"Was I that obvious?"

Evidently, her stare wasn't as good as she'd thought. She'd have to find a way to up her game.

"Your eyes give away everything you're thinking."

When had she become so transparent? Or was it just this man who seemed to see so much?

"Hey," he said, "it's all right. You're safe now."

She wasn't safe. Not with Doug's goons coming after her. How had her life become such a mess? A few hours ago, she was happily engaged to the most wonderful man in the world. Or so she'd thought. Now she was on the run for her life from that same man. Her world had turned on a dime and was still turning.

It was a nightmare.

She'd faced countless obstacles in her life—

time. Staying one step ahead of the gangs that had tried to recruit her had been a never-ending struggle. Other kids on the street had whispered of the ruthless initiations and severe penalties if one tried to leave the gang. It would have been easy, so easy, to have fallen down that hole, one from which she'd feared she could never crawl out.

A friend had invited her to a party. It turned out that the party was a gang initiation, and the so-called friend earned points by recruiting a new "fish." Hailey had run and hadn't looked back.

Only a determination to make something of herself had saved her from that life.

"I don't know what to do." The last word ended on a sob and she pressed her hands to her eyes. She wasn't normally given to crying, but tonight appeared to be an exception.

He didn't try to talk her out of her tears but, instead, let her cry it out. When she'd finished crying, he pulled a handkerchief from his pocket and handed it to her.

The cowboy gave her time to collect herself, and she swiped at the tears and straightened her shoulders. The effect was probably minimal given that she still wore the oversized coat, but it made her feel better.

She pushed the unwelcome thought that the

custom-made coat had belonged to Doug from her mind and took a small pleasure in knowing he was probably livid over its loss. A hollow laugh tickled the back of her throat as she recalled how he'd preened in front of the mirror for no less than forty-five minutes on first receiving the coat.

Get it together, girl. You're running for your life. You don't have time to think about Doug's vanity.

"Something made you smile," he said.

"This coat."

"The coat made you smile?"

"It belongs to my…my husband. It's custom-made. From Italy, no less. He loved this coat. Far more than he ever did me." Why hadn't she seen that before now? Doug loved his possessions. She was but one more possession, someone who looked good on his arm. Someone he could order about and feel important because he could.

Another straightening of her shoulders. Never again would she allow him or anyone else to do that.

She had survived some terrible things. And she'd get through this as well.

"Looks like we're going to be spending some time together," Chap said. "Isn't it about time you told me the truth?"

"The truth?" she echoed.

"You've been lying to me from the beginning. Let's start with your name. Your real name."

He'd seen through her lies, and now she had to make a decision. He'd proved that he was on her side, but could she trust him with the truth?

THREE

"Hailey. Hailey Davenport."

"That's a good start. Now tell me the rest of it."

She lifted her head and scowled at him. "I'm not married, but I am engaged. Or I was until I saw my fiancé kill a man tonight. Those men work for him. Doug sent them to kill me." The tilt of her chin dared him to call her a liar.

The flat words were all the more compelling for their lack of emotion.

"Do you believe me?" she asked after several moments had passed.

"Yes," he said slowly. "I think I do. Did you go to the police?"

"I was going to, but got derailed."

"How so?" Chap found himself more and more intrigued with her story.

"I hid in a car while Doug's men were looking for me. I didn't realize he'd be using it until he and one of his goons climbed inside. They drove all the way from The Point of the Mountain to town, with me hiding under his coat in the back seat. I heard them talking about Doug and the police chief being old friends. He has a lot of powerful friends," she added, the bitterness in her words telling its own story.

"You keep saying 'Doug.' What's his full name?"

"Douglas Lawson."

Chap whistled through his teeth. The name sent off all kinds of alarm bells in his head. "*The* Douglas Lawson? The one that owns half the state and controls the rest of it?"

"That's the one." Her laugh rang hollow. "It felt like I was holding my breath all the way into town, wondering when they'd find me."

"You have a lot of guts."

Another of those laughs that held not a trace of humor. "If that was true, I would have marched into the police station behind Doug and demanded that someone hear me out. As it was, I crawled away like a dog with its tail between its legs." When she looked at him once more, her eyes were filled with regret. "I shouldn't have involved you in my mess. If he finds out that you helped me, he'll make you sorry."

Chap ignored that. "What did you do after that?"

"I hitched a ride to the truck stop. The rest, you know."

He was about to respond when the blare of a siren and flashing lights interrupted the night. He didn't like it. It was too much of a coincidence, but he pulled over and waited. "Stay in the truck."

A squad car pulled in behind them.

Chap didn't get out, only watched two policemen approach his truck. As they got nearer, he took a better look at them. Nothing gave him cause for alarm. Short-cropped hair. Winter-gear uniforms. Still, something about them caused the hair at the back of his neck to stand at attention.

It was then that they opened fire. "Get down on the floor." Bullets pinged off his pickup as he pressed his foot on the gas and took off, leaving the two officers in his rearview mirror.

Whether they were dirty cops or men impersonating real cops, it didn't matter. All that mattered was putting a whole lot of gone between him and Hailey and the would-be killers.

He slanted a look in her direction. "We got away, but make no mistake about it. They will keep coming."

"I know." From the hard note in her voice, he understood that she had no delusions about them having made a clean escape.

When the truck abruptly stopped after about twenty or so miles, he pulled over and then hit the steering wheel with a resounding smack. A bullet must have hit the gas tank, causing it to leak without his knowledge.

He got out, rounded the truck, and saw three bullet holes smack-dab in the middle of the tank. He returned to the cab and lifted the lady out, steadying her until she got her bearings,

True to his training, Sam remained silent while they were being shot at and stayed where he was until Chap said, "Sam, down."

Sam bounded out of the truck.

Red and blue lights speared the night, signaling that the shooters were close.

Chap grabbed her hand. "We've got to run for it," he said, feeling the ancient instinct of fight or flight kick in as adrenaline flooded his body.

Though he was armed, he suspected their pursuers were loaded for bear, with extra firepower at the ready. He couldn't make a stand here, not with Hailey at his side. If he'd been alone, he'd have risked it; he could take care of himself. But he couldn't protect her and take out two heavily armed tangos at the same time.

He spared a moment to check his phone and wasn't surprised that there were no bars. This area often lost bars during a storm. Okay. They were on their own.

They plunged into the woods, Sam leading the way. The heavy snow made for slow going.

Hailey's long dress and high-heeled sandals weren't in any way suited to tramping through the ankle-deep snow. It didn't help that the coat dragged the ground with every step, further slowing her progress.

Chap kept moving, sometimes dragging, sometimes pulling her along, until he accepted she couldn't go any farther. He had to find somewhere safe to stash her while he dealt with the men chasing them.

Sam ran ahead then returned. Chap knew he was searching out any sense of threat.

He lowered his head so that she could hear him over the wind's bluster. "I'm going to put you somewhere safe."

Even in the stingy amount of moonlight available, he could see her eyes grow wide with alarm. "What are you going to do?"

"Take them out," he said with no fanfare, only grim determination.

"There're two of them and only one of you." Her words came out in a panicked whisper. Her voice shook, and he knew it wasn't all because of the cold.

He found a hollowed-out tree, probably

damaged from a fire. It would offer both shelter from the storm and a hiding place. "I'll be all right. The important thing is that you stay hidden. Got it?"

"Got it."

"You'll be safe here. Sam will take care of you. Just keep still. I'll be back." He saw the flicker of fear in her eyes. "That's a promise." He turned to Sam. "Stay, boy. Take care of the lady."

Sam gave a mournful whine that he wasn't invited along, but he hunkered down near the woman.

"Be safe," she whispered.

After she and Sam were tucked inside the tree, Chap did his best to brush away any tracks.

He didn't doubt that he could take out the two men. He wasn't given to boasting, but neither did he downplay his skills. As one of his SEAL instructors had said, "It ain't bragging if you can back it up."

He was in stealth mode now, slowing his breathing until it scarcely lifted his chest. With the sliver of light that had worked its way between the trees, he found a set of tracks. Only one, though. The men must have separated.

Okay. He'd take them out one at a time. He

wished he'd had Sam with him, but he couldn't leave Hailey on her own.

He followed the tracks and was rewarded when he heard the thump of heavy footfalls. His quarry was tramping about with little regard to the noise he was making, a sure sign that he wasn't a professional, only a hired gun. In his experience, hired guns didn't have a stake in the outcome of a mission and were more easily eliminated.

As silent as the man was loud, Chap moved up behind him, employed a hard chop to his neck and took him down. He collapsed with scarcely a sound. Chap eyed the man's heavy police-issued jacket. Though Chap knew Hailey wouldn't want anything from the men chasing her, she needed warmth. He undid the man's jacket and slipped it from his shoulders.

As he did so, his eyes narrowed. A bullet hole occupied dead center of the back of the jacket. It didn't take much reasoning to deduce that the men had killed two cops and taken their uniforms. He'd do his best to make sure she didn't see the grim sight of the hole.

Using the man's belt, Chap bound his hands. He then undid the man's shoes and removed them, intending to bring them back for Hailey. He didn't concern himself about the man getting cold. His lips hardened in a taut line as he pictured the coward shooting a cop in the back.

He straightened in preparation for taking out the second killer. He was an apex predator. His prey would never see him coming.

Hailey prayed. For Chap's safety as well as her own.

Her feet had grown numb, but she dared not stomp them for fear of giving away her location. As though sensing that she needed his body heat as well as his comfort, Sam huddled closer to her.

Shivers trembled through her, followed by pinpricks of pain as the cold enveloping her grew more and more intense. When the pain ceased, she was at first relieved but then recognized it for what it was: she was dangerously close to hypothermia. Even knowing that, she wanted nothing more than to let sleep claim her, the most dangerous thing she could do.

Despite the cold, she was sweating profusely, from the effort of running through the woods and now from sheer terror. One of the first rules in surviving extreme cold was to avoid exertion that caused the body to sweat. Sweat would freeze on the body and encourage her body temperature to drop even more rapidly.

She wished she could talk with Sam, but that wasn't possible, not without betraying her hiding place. She contented herself by patting his head.

Even worse than the cold was the waiting. And the wondering. Would Chap return? He had sounded confident that he could take out the men chasing them, but despite his skills, it didn't change the fact that there were two men to his one. Besides, what did she know about him?

Just when she thought she couldn't bear the cold and the worry another moment, a crunching sound warned that she wasn't alone. Sam's fur bristled, telling her that he heard it also.

If it had been Chap, he would have called out.

No, this had to be one of the men after her, and though Chap had told her to stay put, she couldn't remain where she was, prey to one or both of the men pursuing her. She would be at their mercy if they found her. She slipped from her hiding spot, found a branch and held it like a bat.

Sam gave a low-pitched growl.

Chap had said that the big shepherd would protect her, but she couldn't risk being dependent on him. Her heartbeat sounding deafeningly loud to her ears, she put a hand to her chest, even while recognizing the foolishness of the gesture.

She wasn't some weak-kneed wimp who squealed when she saw a mouse. *She could do this.*

When she heard footsteps nearing the tree, her hands tightened on the branch, but she didn't make her move. Not yet. Instead, she waited. A huff of heavy breathing told her he was almost upon her. A heartbeat later, she wielded the branch and connected with something solid. She'd hit him, but he wasn't out.

A knee to the groin sent him to his knees. The fury in his eyes caused her to want to take a step back, but she held her ground.

"Do your thing, Sam," she said, not certain how to give orders to the dog.

He leaped on the man and grabbed his arm, large jaws clamping.

"Get him off me," her would-be attacker cried.

"I'd suggest you not struggle. Sam may take it as a sign that he should bite down harder."

If Chap had taken out the other one, they were home free. But if he hadn't…

She couldn't know and had to be prepared. Being proactive felt good. She refused to be a victim any longer.

When Sam went on alert again, still holding

on to his captive's arm, she knew someone else was coming and hefted her branch once more.

Before she realized what was happening, she was quickly disarmed from behind. She scratched and clawed before she recognized the voice.

"It's all right. It's me."

Chap.

He looked at her, then at Sam, and finally the man cowering on the ground. A grin stretched across his face. "You and Sam make a pretty good team."

"Mister, make him let me go." The man was practically whimpering. "He's nearly chewing my arm off."

Chap ignored him. "Good job," he said to her and Sam. "Both of you."

Hailey felt bound to give credit where credit was due. "Sam did most of the work."

Chap ignored that and said, "Take off your coat."

Puzzled, she could only stare at him. He wanted her to take off the coat in the middle of a blizzard? Had the extreme cold affected his thinking? She was still trying to make sense of his words when he held up a jacket. He then helped her take off the snow-soaked coat and tossed it to the ground.

"Now hold out your arms." As he said the

words, he slipped a jacket over her shoulders. So cold was she that she couldn't make her arms work. He helped her tuck her arms into the sleeves, then zipped up the jacket when her fingers fumbled.

Warmth. Wonderful, blissful warmth. She sank into it.

"Where did you find it?" And then it hit her. He must have taken it from the other man.

She wanted to reject the jacket, but practicality took over. For the last several hours, she'd been wearing Doug's coat; why should she object to wearing the jacket of one of his men? If she was to survive, she needed to get her body temperature up. The coat she'd taken from her one-time fiancé wasn't waterproof and was now soaking wet.

"Thank you." She was shivering so badly that she barely got the words out.

"No problem. Let's make sure the tango you and Sam took out stays put."

Sam hadn't let up on the man's arm and looked like he could keep it up all night. Apparently, his captive felt the same because he was close to blubbering.

Chap looked at him in disgust and then said, "Sam. Release."

The dog let go of the arm but remained on alert.

Hailey frowned over the unfamiliar word. "'Tango'?"

"Military-speak for bad guy." He gave the first man's shoes to Hailey. "They won't fit, but they'll be better than what you're wearing." He then undid the man's belt and used it to bind his hands. "He won't be going anywhere anytime soon."

"That's a pretty neat trick," she said as she stuffed her feet into the big shoes. Chap was right. They were better—a whole lot better—than the evening slippers she'd been wearing.

He flashed a cocky grin. "SEALs learn to make do."

She wasn't surprised to learn he'd been a navy SEAL. "I know something about making do. Ask me sometime about my ramen days." She worked up a smile, but it felt stiff, like her lips didn't want to cooperate.

Neither did her hands as she worked to clasp and unclasp them in a vain attempt to get feeling back into her fingers. When her legs threatened to buckle beneath her, she knew she was in trouble.

Big trouble.

It was taking too long.

Chap had checked his phone and found that it showed two bars, enough to text his foreman, Dinkum, and arrange for a pick-up. Fortunately, they weren't too far from his ranch. He had turned to Hailey, wanting to share the good news, but the words had died on his lips.

Her lips were colorless. Worse, she wheezed with every breath, her chest and shoulders lifting in an uneven rhythm as she struggled to take in air and then expel it.

He suspected both he and Hailey were riding an adrenaline high, but the letdown would come soon enough, leaving them even colder than they had been. He would survive it better than she would, given she lacked the muscle mass and the experience in dealing with the aftermath of an adrenaline burn.

The road. He focused on that. All they had to do was make it as far as the road.

No problem.

Except that he didn't think she'd make it.

He needed to get her warmed up. With that uppermost in his mind, he urged her to walk faster. Sam kept pace with them, body vibrating with impatience at the slow stride.

Chap took Hailey's elbow and helped her over some fallen branches. She needed to generate body heat. Maybe talking would help to keep her moving. "Tell me how you got involved with Lawson."

An off-the-wall question to ask as they plodded through the woods, it was all he could come up with.

"I catered a party he attended. He liked what I'd done and asked me to cater one of his business events. He was handsome, charming, and intelligent. When he asked me out, I couldn't believe it. I didn't know who he was, just that he was nice and seemed to like me." Her speech slowed with every word. "We dated for several months, and I fell in love with him. When he asked me to marry him, I said yes. He was every girl's dream. Or so I'd thought."

He heard the regret in her words. Regret and puzzlement. He didn't blame her. Douglas Lawson was one of the most powerful men in the West, with interests in mining, technology, engineering and entertainment, in addition to backing political candidates.

Word was that he was thinking of running for political office himself. From Chap's time in the marshals, he'd heard about Lawson's involvement in organized crime. Rumors had circulated in the law enforcement community about the man for years, but nothing had ever been pinned on him.

"When I saw him murder that man tonight," she said, "it was a wake-up call."

"How do you mean?"

"Some things had been bothering me for a

while, but I dismissed them, thinking I'd misunderstood their meaning."

"What kinds of things?"

"Secret meetings. People coming to the door in the middle of the night. It wasn't like…you know. I had my own suite in his house. Doug said he wanted to keep his business competitors from knowing what he was doing and that's why the middle-of-the-night meetings. He's a very important man," she added.

The naïveté of the statement would have made him smile if the circumstances had been different. Maybe that very innocence had protected her, prevented her from seeing what Lawson really was until now.

"Did you meet many of his friends?"

"A few. At the parties he gave. They never spent much time talking with me. They weren't interested in his little caterer fiancée." Another flush. "I was out of my depth with them, and mostly stayed in the background. Their wives didn't much like me, either, but put up with me because I was Doug's fiancée."

Chap could picture it. A bunch of snobs, looking down their noses on anyone who didn't belong to their social circle and actually worked for a living.

Abruptly, she stopped in her tracks. Had talking taken too much from her?

They couldn't afford to remain still, not with the wind and cold cutting through them, lethal knives slicing into flesh.

He had to keep her moving. Though he knew the jacket helped, she was still shivering uncontrollably. That, plus her speech and the way her hands and fingers had fumbled, told him she was in the danger zone for hypothermia.

With an arm around her waist, he started walking again. "What did you do after you saw him shoot the man?"

"At first, I just stared. When I tried to get out of their sight, I stumbled. Doug and his men heard me. He called to me, and when I didn't answer, he sent the men after me."

"What did you do then?"

"I ran."

The bald statement said everything.

Every syllable came out in little puffs of air. It wasn't that that concerned him. It was the slowness of her speech, as though she was searching for the words. Hypothermia could rob a person of the ability to talk or even think. In addition, she had stopped shivering. Not a good sign. Not a good sign at all.

Chap pressed her to walk faster, but ice-laden branches and deep snow had slowed their pace to a crawl. Even so, Hailey couldn't keep up, as though the last bit of talking had drained her of any remaining energy.

She faltered with each step, her breathing growing more and more labored, and he knew she was reaching the end of her endurance.

"Want to sleep," she mumbled.

Sleep was the worst thing for someone going into hypothermia.

"No sleeping." He made his voice sharp, wanting to shock her out of the lethargy quickly overtaking her. "Not yet."

"'Kay.'"

"Hailey, listen. We have to keep moving. If we stop, we'll freeze to death." When she didn't answer, he gave her a gentle shake and said, "Sam won't leave us. You don't want him to freeze, do you?"

"I like Sam. He's nice." Then she giggled.

The slow speech, out-of-place laughter, and loss of motor dexterity all said she was succumbing to the extreme cold.

His phone pinged, signaling an incoming text. A glance at it told him it was Dinkum saying he was at the coordinates Chap had given him.

He weighed getting Hailey to the truck as quickly as possible against the danger of carrying her the rest of the way and allowing her to sleep. Enough was enough. He scooped her up in his arms.

"Can't carry me," she protested.

"I've carried injured buddies who are a lot bigger than you." Running twenty miles while carrying a ninety-pound pack wasn't an unusual exercise for SEALs. It'd be no problem at all to carry her. The only problem was to get her out of the cold in time.

She laid her head on his shoulder. And sighed.

When he heard her breathing even out, he knew she was giving in to sleep.

Hurry.

FOUR

When they reached the ranch house after a short drive, he carried Hailey inside. Though he'd have preferred having her checked out at the hospital, his ranch was closer. He'd treated enough people with hypothermia to know what to look for and how to care for them.

Mrs. Heppel, his housekeeper, bustled out. "Poor girl," the woman said with one look at Hailey's pale face and bedraggled clothes. Though she wasn't unconscious, she was clearly at the end of her energy. "Don't you worry about her. I'll find some clothes to fit her. We'll set her up for the night." She tsked over Chap. "You take care of yourself. I'll see to the lady."

Though he was dead-tired and longed for a hot shower and a hot meal, he couldn't just hand Hailey over without making sure that she was going to be all right. "Help her into some dry clothes. I'll heat up some soup for the two of us." His housekeeper always kept a pot of soup simmering on the stove during the winter months.

Relieved that Hailey was in good hands, he headed to his room, took a quick shower, then hurried back downstairs. In the kitchen, he ladled soup into bowls and toasted thick slices of homemade bread in the oven.

Mrs. Heppel appeared then. "The lady won't be joining you. She went right to sleep after I got her into some dry clothes."

"Thanks for seeing to her."

Eating because his body needed it, not because he was hungry, he reviewed the events of the night. *What have I gotten himself into?*

After finishing his meal, he went to bed and lay there, thinking again about what had happened, before giving into a deep exhaustion.

The following morning, Chap checked on Hailey before starting his day. He found her sleeping, her breathing normal, which reassured him. She'd been worn out last night and needed all the rest she could get.

Reassured that she was all right, he headed to the barn. Chores still had to be done; fences still had to be repaired; animals still had to be fed. The work went on, no matter that he had an unexpected houseguest, and though he had men who could take care of the chores, he liked to keep a hand in.

Besides, it was Christmas Day. He couldn't handle everything himself for the entire day, but he could spare some time to let the men have a couple of hours off.

What had he been thinking, bringing a woman to the ranch? That was the problem. He hadn't been thinking. He'd seen the stark fear in her eyes, the plea for help, and he'd been lost. His buddies in the SEALs had called it a hero complex. All he'd known was that he couldn't abandon her.

*Didn't he have enough problems?*Dinkum managed the place when he wasn't here. Chap trusted his friend to take care of the place as he himself would. Fortunately, his arrangement with S&J permitted him to make trips to the ranch when he needed to get away. He had a place in Denver but felt confined there, and he missed the open spaces. Living in the city seemed to be a series of big steps and little steps, none of them taking him anywhere.

Honesty forced him to admit that it wasn't the ranch that needed him but, rather, he who needed it. He needed the routine, the work, backbreaking as it was, to take his mind from Lori's murder. Finding the murderer hadn't erased the pain as he'd hoped. Instead, it had only intensified his grief because he had no-where else to direct his anger.

He'd told himself he didn't want vengeance but justice. However, his self-imposed mission to bring the man in had fallen perilously close to the former. The peace he'd sought had eluded him and continued to do so.

Peace was in short supply in today's world. What made him think he deserved it when so many others were denied it? The fact was, he had no more claim on peace than anyone else.

Dinkum found him in the barn. "Thought you'd be here. Boss, what are you mixed up in?" The baldness of the statement caused Chap's lips to quirk at the corners.

"I was just wondering that myself."

"You wanna tell me what's going on?"

Chap had shared the bare bones of Hailey's story with his foreman last night, but clearly his friend wanted more.

Another man might have taken offense at being questioned, but Chap and Dink went way back. They'd served in the SEALs together, though Dinkum was ten years older and had taken a medical discharge. During a raid on the enemy's cache of weapons, he had lost partial use of his left eye.

The two men had stayed in touch, and when Chap had bought the ranch, he'd recruited Dinkum to join him. The arrangement had worked out for both of them, with Dinkum acting as boss when Chap was absent.

The former SEAL didn't put up with nonsense and made certain the ranch ran as smoothly when Chap was in Colorado on assignment for S&J as it did when he was there. He chuckled to himself. Dinkum no doubt could claim the ranch ran more smoothly when he was in charge. He could be right.

Chap told him the rest of what Hailey had shared with him.

The foreman gave a low whistle. "She sure got herself mixed up with a skunk. I don't know all that much about Lawson, but I've heard enough to know to that he's a bad one clean to the bone."

"Tell me what you've heard."

Dinkum had a circle of ex-military types who kept him up to date on what was going on in this part of Wyoming and Colorado. His friends had proved invaluable in Chap's work for S&J.

When Chap had asked him why he did what he did, Dinkum had replied that while he may have left the SEALs and the war on terrorism, he was still in the battle of good versus evil. There were plenty of bad guys out there who needed to be taken down, he'd claimed, and he was happy to oblige.

Chap understood. He'd seen enough injustices during his time in the SEALs to last a lifetime. That hadn't changed when he'd returned stateside and worked for the US Marshals, then S&J. Anytime you could do something to right a wrong, you seized upon it and did your best to make things just.

"He's got his fingers in every dirty business out there. Drugs. Prostitution. Money laundering. Human trafficking. He owns several newspapers and television stations, which give him a lot of power in shaping public opinion. Altogether, it makes for a nasty mix."

Chap slanted a grin at his friend. "You know a lot for not knowing much."

Dinkum nodded in a way he'd probably intended to be modest but held not a speck of modesty in it. "You know me. I keep my ear to the ground."

"I need to keep Hailey safe," Chap said. "She's all alone."

Dinkum sent a sly look his way. "She's awfully pretty."

"I hadn't noticed." That was a lie. Of course he'd noticed. Any man would have. With blond hair and deep green eyes, she was beautiful, even last night with her hair matted from the sleet and snow and her face splattered with mud. But it wasn't only her looks that attracted him; Hailey intrigued him more than he was comfortable admitting.

A harrumph was Dinkum's only response. Chap supposed he deserved that.

"What are you going to do with her?"

"I don't know. I've got to find out what the lady wants."

"Besides staying alive?" Dinkum asked dryly.

"Yeah. Besides that. I have a couple of ideas. How are the meals since you and the boys started cooking for yourselves?"

Dinkum lifted his brow at the out-of-left-field question. His snort answered the question. "Don't joke about food. We've been eating out of cans for the most part."

Chap nodded, a tentative plan taking shape in his head. After finishing the chores, he returned to the main house while Dinkum headed to the bunkhouse.

Christmas morning.

At one time, the ranch house had been decorated elaborately for the season. Even the bunkhouse had received its share of attention. The rich scent of roasted turkey and baked ham had filled the air.

There were no decorations now, no smells

of Christmas cookies or savory treats. Though the men celebrated on their own, Christmas was just another day for Chap. Scratch that. It was a day to get through, to endure the painful memories it carried. With the habit of long practice, he shoved them away and focused on what needed to be done now.

In his office, he did a computer search on Hailey's fiancé. The man owned restaurants, sports centers, even laundromats. That seemed innocuous enough, but those businesses were all good places to launder money, a necessity when you had cash pouring in from dozens of illegal activities. He had never paid much attention to the media coverage of Lawson, but he'd read enough to know that the man had his fingers in a number of businesses.

He needed more and made a call to Josh Harvath at S&J. He asked him to do a run on Lawson, determine if any connection had been made between him and a recent murder in Fort Collins.

The colleague he trusted most, Rafe Zuniga, was away for the holidays with his wife, Shannon, and their twin daughters. He was loathe to call other S&J colleagues who were likely busy with family. Josh would come through for him, even though it was Christmas Day. He was as much a loner as was Chap.

When Harvath got back to him, Chap's concern deepened. "Not only couldn't I find any connection between Lawson and a murder, I couldn't even get a whiff of a murder last night."

"Thanks, buddy. I appreciate you making the time for this."

Had the police not found the body yet? Were they still processing the crime scene? Or was it a cover-up? With Lawson's resources, he could easily have made it disappear.

If the murder had been hushed up, it meant that Lawson had put pressure on people in high places. What *had* he gotten himself mixed up in? Chap wondered, echoing Dinkum's question.

It was too late now.

The lady clearly needed help and he couldn't turn her out. The crime had taken place in Colorado, not Wyoming. More importantly, if Hailey was right and Lawson did have law enforcement connections, Chap could place her in more danger by going to the feds. It wouldn't be the first time the police, both local and federal, had been bought off.

Of course, he could go to the local authorities. Victoria "Vic" Crane was sheriff of the small town and everything surrounding it for a hundred miles in each direction. The sheriff's office couldn't afford to hire sufficient deputies to cover such a large area, so Crane occasionally deputized ranchers and cowhands when needed, like breaking up a fight in a bar or pulling a car out of a snowbank.

Chap had filled in on more than one occasion. He liked Vic. She was as proficient with a gun as she was with her fists, and though she preferred talking people down from doing something foolish, she had used both when circumstances called for it. There wasn't a man in the county who didn't respect her, and, in some instances, fear her.

He considered the idea of taking Hailey to Vic and explaining the story, but he wasn't ready to do that. Not yet. For one thing, Vic would be obligated to go to the authorities if she had knowledge that he was harboring a witness to a murder. For another, Vic had made some fairly obvious hints that she wanted to be more than friends with him, and he didn't want to go down that road.

With friends at S&J and in law enforcement, he had others he could call on, but he was somehow reluctant to do so. Could it be because *he* wanted to be the one to take care of Hailey? Because *he* wanted to show that he could be responsible for keeping a woman safe?

It was time he talked with his houseguest.

He found her sitting at the kitchen table, nursing a cup of hot chocolate.

She gestured to a plate of Christmas cookies. "I hope you don't mind. I raided your pantry and found the makings for cookies and hot chocolate."

He stiffened for a moment at the sight of the merrily decorated cookies and then put aside the feelings they stirred in him.

He bit into one. "I don't mind at all. Mind if I share them with the boys?"

"I already gave a plate to Mrs. Heppel to give to the men."

Imagining their reactions, he grinned.

His grin died as he thought of how he'd ignored Christmas this year and the last. In the past, the ranch had rang with laughter during the holidays. The dining room table and that of the bunkhouse had groaned under the weight of turkey, ham, and all that went with them.

"I noticed that there wasn't a tree or any decorations," she said softly. "Did I do something wrong in making Christmas cookies?"

"No." He looked at her closely. Though she looked okay, there was a shell-shocked glaze in her eyes, like she didn't know what to do next.

He didn't blame her. In the last twelve hours, she'd been through an ordeal that would have broken many people, witnessing her fiancé murder someone and then running for her life.

He took a chair opposite her. "We need to talk about what happens next."

She braced her shoulders as though preparing for bad news.

"I'll help you in any way I can, but I need to know what *you* want to do. If you want to go to the authorities, I'll take you. I know the sheriff here in town. She'll know what to do. But if you want to stay here and get your bearings for a few days, that's fine."

"I don't know. Hearing Doug is all buddy-buddy with the police chief makes me wonder if I should just keep running." When Chap started to voice his concern, she held up a hand. "I know that's not the right thing. Or even the safe thing. But right now, I don't think I can face being questioned by the police. Why should they believe me over the mighty Douglas Lawson?"

She had a good point. "I get it. If that's the case, I have an idea."

She leaned forward expectantly.

"You said that you're a caterer."

She sent him a cautious look. "That's right."

"How would you feel about cooking for the men in return for room and board and salary?"

Her eyes widened. "Do you mean it?"

He nodded. "The men have been eating their own cooking for a year. From what I hear, they're sick of it."

She inhaled sharply. The glazed look in her eyes faded, to be replaced by a cautious pleasure. "That would be wonderful. If you're serious—"

"I am. I've got twelve men who are always hungry. They work hard and need good food and lots of it. If you can keep them happy, you'll be doing me a favor. If your cooking tastes as good as these cookies do, the men will bow down and kiss your feet."

A smile lit her face. "It sounds perfect. Thank you."

Chap wondered if he had just made the biggest mistake of his life. He had his own problems; he didn't need to be taking on anyone else's. But the gratitude on her face touched a long-forgotten place in his heart. She needed him.

No one had needed him in a long time.

On her first day of work, the day after Christmas, Hailey was determined to show Chap and his men what she could do. She'd spent most of the previous day familiarizing herself with the bunkhouse's huge kitchen. It boasted everything she would need and then some.

When Chap had introduced her to the men and said she'd be cooking for them, they'd greeted her with a tepid welcome. After learning that she was the one who'd made the holiday cookies, they'd brightened.

Now, stirring a huge bowl of pancake batter, she felt her thoughts spin. She'd resolved to put the murder out of her mind, at least for today, but she couldn't help reliving the disbelief and subsequent terror of seeing her fiancé murder a man.

Over the years, she'd seen dozens of television shows and movies of witnesses on the run to escape wicked villains. Never had she thought she would find herself in that position.

If not for Chap, she wouldn't be on the run. She'd be dead.

Not for the first time, she asked herself how she could have been so wrong about Doug.

During the next few days, Hailey learned about cooking for ranch hands. She learned that she had to double or even triple the amount she would normally make. She learned that the men asking for "seconds" was a given. And she'd learned that a good belch was a compliment. Finally, she'd learned that the noon meal was called dinner while the evening meal was supper.

The lukewarm welcome the men had first given her had turned to full-out cheers. In no time at all, Hailey was happier than she could remember being. Looking back, she realized those months with Doug hadn't been so much happy as a respite from loneliness.

Cooking for the ranch hands was satisfying in a way her catering work had never been. It had taken a few meals to get the knack of cooking the kind of food that the men liked and in sufficient quantities, but now she felt at ease and was rewarded with their frequent requests for seconds.

Only one man gave her pause. Bob Klaverly. She didn't like the way he eyed her with something akin to speculation. She chalked it up to the trauma of witnessing a murder and did her best to put her uneasiness out of her mind. No way was she going to run to Chap and tell him that she didn't like the way a man was looking at her.

Determined to make a special supper since it was Saturday night, she roasted chicken, complete with rosemary stuffing and new potatoes. The aroma wafted through the kitchen and into the rest of the bunkhouse. There was peach cobbler, served with plenty of whipped cream, for dessert.

Dark came early and, with it, such intense cold that the air was brittle. It rushed in when the men stomped inside from completing the evening chores.

When Chap wandered in, sniffing appreciatively, she smiled in greeting. "Hi. Are you thinking of joining us this evening?"

She'd learned that Chap typically ate by himself in his office, but on more than one occasion lately, he'd joined the men in the bunkhouse kitchen.

"I don't have to ask how you like the work. You look happy."

She didn't have to think about it. "I love it. It's a lot more fun than cooking for fussy society ladies who want the latest thing and then refuse to eat it because they might gain an ounce."

He pulled a face. "Sounds rough."

"It was." She spread her hands to encompass the enormous kitchen and dining hall. "Here, I can cook for people who will actually eat what I make and like it. It's perfect."

The moment the words were out, she wanted to snatch them back, and prayed he hadn't taken them the wrong way.

She knew this time at the ranch was just

a respite; she couldn't stay here forever. But the knowledge that she was safe, if only for a short while, went a long way to soothe her pent-up fear. Gratitude poured through her. The Lord had put Chap in her path just when she'd needed him most.

"I'd join you every night, but your cooking will make it so that I can't fit in my jeans."

She looked at his trim, muscular build and laughed. "I don't think you have to worry."

"Maybe you need to start serving carrot and celery sticks, though I don't know how it would go over with the men."

She laughed, appreciating his humor. The laughter died in her throat as she thought of Doug, whose idea of humor was cutting sarcasm.

Hailey snuck another glance at Chap, taking in the rugged lines of his face. Another time, another place, she would have been attracted, but nothing could happen between them.

That was fine by her. The last thing she was looking for was a man in her life, not even one as appealing as Chap.

The following night, Chap was finishing up the monthly taxes. He had put off the paperwork that seemed to multiply overnight for as long as he could. When had he become an accountant instead of a rancher?

He decided he deserved a break. Maybe he'd wander over to the bunkhouse and see what Hailey was serving for supper.

When Dinkum showed up, Chap tensed. He knew from the way his friend shifted his hat from one hand to the other that something was wrong.

"What's up?"

"Two dudes showed up at the far gate. They said they were lost and asked for directions back to town. Thing is, their truck was brand-new, should have GPS on it, so why did they need directions?"

Why indeed?

"Anything else bother you?"

"The way they were dressed. Jeans so new you could practically hear the denim cracking. Pointy-toe boots that no one who knows better would buy. Big hats that were all for show.

"They were as out of place as I'd be at a tea party with fancy cakes and china cups."

Chap cracked a smile at the image, though he was feeling far from amused. "What'd you do?"

"I sent them packing."

"Did they ask about Hailey?"

"No. But they sure were looking the place over."

"Thanks, Dink. You did the right thing."

It wasn't uncommon for travelers to get lost, stumble upon the ranch and ask for directions. It didn't mean the men were necessarily there looking for Hailey. Despite his attempts to reassure himself that Hailey was not the reason for the men's presence, he knew better. Lawson's men obviously had a lead that she was in the area. They may not know her exact location, but that didn't mean they wouldn't find out.

In spite of the vast spaces, it was a small community in terms of neighbors knowing what was going on with each other. He knew he couldn't keep Hailey hidden forever on the ranch. Word was bound to leak out that he had a pretty lady cooking for the men, but he'd do what it took to keep her presence on the down-low for as long as possible.

"Are you going to tell the men what's going on?" Dinkum asked.

Chap nodded. The ranch hands had already noticed that he had assigned men to guard duty. Normally, they relied on fences and riding them during the day to keep out animals and trespassers, but he'd felt the need to increase security.

"They need to know what they might be facing. If they don't want to stay, I get it."

He hadn't told them what had brought Hailey to the ranch, but they were shrewd enough to understand that she was in some kind of trouble. It said a lot about her that they kept a protective watch over her.

Both he and Dinkum headed to the bunkhouse. It was suppertime, and all of the men but the two doing fence duty would be there in the kitchen.

He took a few moments to watch as Hailey went about preparing the meal. The economy of her movements, the sure way she set about assembling her ingredients, convinced him he'd made the right choice in offering her the job. When tantalizing aromas filled the air, he grinned.

"You're spoiling the men," he told her now.

Her smile came easily, turning her eyes soft. "It's just plain fare."

"It's a lot more than that. I hear what they're saying. They're even getting cleaned up for supper. That's a first."

The blush on her cheeks was adorable.

"The men are sweet."

Chap guffawed with laughter over that. "Don't let them hear you say that. They'll be so embarrassed that they'll never show their faces outside the bunkhouse again."

"Because I called them sweet?"

The puzzled look in her eyes was as adorable as the blush on her cheeks. He needed to shut up before he did something foolish like tell her *she* was adorable.

Which reminded him why he'd come to the kitchen in the first place.

He caught Dinkum's eye and knew he couldn't put off sharing the news with her any longer.

"Dinkum spotted two men at the fence. They asked a couple of questions then went on their way."

"Do you think they work for Lawson?"

"I don't know. But I can't dismiss it."

"How were they dressed?" she asked.

"Like dudes." *Dude* meant a city person trying to dress Western, and was often openly scoffed at by the locals.

"Am I a dude?"

"No way. You look like a real ranch hand now." He reached out to dab at her face, his finger coming away with a smudge of flour. "Dink and I are doing our best to keep you safe, but I think it's time we let the men in on what's going on. That okay with you?"

"I wouldn't blame them for wanting me to leave. They didn't sign up for this," she said.

"Let's ask them."

With Hailey at his side, he briefed the men on what was going on, including the two strangers showing up at the front gate, and was gratified when, to a man, they stood by Hailey.

"Nobody's gonna hurt Miss Hailey," one said.

Before the others could add their agreement, an alarm sounded, and one of the ranch hands who had night duty burst in the doorway. "Boss, the barn is on fire."

Fire, even in the winter months, spelled disaster for a working ranch. Bales of hay, wooden fences, all made fodder for hungry flames.

"Stay here!" Chap barked at Hailey. "Dink, stay with her."

"I can help," she said.

"No! This could be a trick to get you out in the open."

He gave Dinkum a hard look and took off.

The scene that greeted him had him biting down hard on his anger. There'd be time enough for that later. More than the horrific sight of the fire eating through everything in its path, though, were the sounds. Terrified cries from the horses pierced the night.

He started into the barn when one of the men clamped a hand over his arm. "Boss, you can't go in there."

"I won't let them burn."

He ripped off his jacket and draped it over his head. And ran into the flames.

FIVE

Hailey turned to Dinkum. "What's going on?"

"You heard same as me. Fire. If you want to help, start making thermoses of coffee. The men are going to need something warm in their bellies."

With Mrs. Heppel's help, she made gallon after gallon of coffee, along with dozens of sandwiches. Two hours later, they were still at it. The housekeeper yawned widely and, seeing the weariness in her eyes, Hailey suggested she go upstairs.

When a couple of men staggered in, she poured two cups and handed them over. "How is it?" she asked.

"Bad," one said, "but the boss saved the horses. The sounds they made…" He shook his head. "I never want to hear those again."

She sent thermoses with the men, along with four sacks of sandwiches. When another man showed up twenty minutes later, she gave him a sandwich, pressed a cup of coffee into his hands, and sent more coffee and sandwiches with him. While she couldn't physically fight the fire, she could at least make certain the men weren't working on empty stomachs.

Not wanting the meal she'd fixed to go to waste, she put everything in containers and stacked them in the refrigerator. If anyone got hungry in the middle of the night, there'd be plenty of food.

Dinkum excused himself. "Got to answer nature's call," he said.

A cold draft wrapped its way around her as she was cleaning up. She looked over to see the back door to the kitchen ajar. Thinking someone must not have latched it properly, she went to close it but found herself lifted off her feet. Too late, she realized the significance of the open door. If she hadn't been exhausted all the way down to her fingertips, her brain might have made the connection already.

"We're going to take us a little ride," the man holding her said. "Newly, go get the truck and bring it along front." He set her down. "Make a move, and I'll make sure it's your last."

Before she could scream for help, a kerchief was tied over her mouth, and her arms were pulled behind her back and bound, but she wasn't helpless. She kicked back and connected with the man's shin. As she had taken to wearing the cowboy boots she'd borrowed from Mrs. Heppel, she got in a good blow.

Without saying a word, he turned her around and slapped her across the face, sending her to the floor.

Okay, so maybe she'd played that wrong, but she wouldn't let some muscle-for-hire take her without a fight.

He jerked her up and began to push her out of the kitchen when she felt the heavy hand on her shoulder lift.

"Think again," a furious voice said.

She spun to see Dinkum knock the man flat. She tried to warn him that her attacker wasn't alone, but the gag around her mouth reduced her words to gibberish. The foreman yanked the man up by his jacket, prepared to hit him again, when he was slammed from behind.

The one called Newly had returned. He now held the foreman's arms while the other man hit him in the face and gut.

Footsteps sounded just beyond the door.

"She was supposed to be alone while everybody was seeing to the fire," Newly said on a whine. "Let's get out of here."

Both men fled.

Dinkum charged after them. By that time,

two of the ranch hands had discovered the ruckus.

"The boss sent us in to get coffee," Pete, the youngest of the workers, said as he pulled away her gag and undid the rope binding her hands. The other, Bob Klaverly, stood by and watched, his expression one of speculation.

"I'm gonna get the boss," Pete said. He returned within minutes.

Chap took in the scene. "What happened?"

"I messed up. Big-time," Dinkum said.

"Don't believe him," Hailey said. "He saved me. If he hadn't come back when he did, they would have taken me." She wet a cloth with cold water and pressed it to the darkening mark on Dinkum's face.

In bits and pieces, the two of them filled Chap in on what happened. Dark with soot and eyes red, his face assumed a grim expression.

"It's my fault," Hailey said quietly. "If it hadn't been for me..."

"Give us the room, please," Chap said to those gathered.

Without a murmur, the others cleared the kitchen.

"I can't stay here."

He brought her to him. "We're both tired and in no shape to make decisions."

She couldn't disagree there.

With that, he cupped her elbow and together they headed back to the main house.

Thoughts swirling, she got ready for bed. When she finally slid between the sheets, though, she didn't sleep, her mind filled with images of burning barns and terrified horses.

Morning did not bring relief from her thoughts. Instead, it clarified them. She couldn't stay here. It wasn't fair or right that she bring this kind of trouble to the ranch.

More by rote than by intention, she started breakfast.

When Chap found her in the kitchen, he took a huge pan of biscuits from her and set it on the butcher-block counter. "The men will make these disappear before you can butter them."

She smiled wanly. "I hope so." She slid the biscuits from the pan and put them on a platter.

"You look like you didn't sleep much," he said.

"No, I didn't. How about you?"

"I was out before I closed my eyes."

"What will you do about the barn?"

"Build again," he said with the resolve she'd come to associate with him. "In the spring. In the meantime, I have an old barn that will do once I have the men shore up the stalls."

"I've been thinking—" But she didn't get any further.

"That you should leave the ranch," he finished for her.

"Yes." She croaked out the word. Leaving the ranch was the last thing she wanted to do, but she didn't have a choice. Because of her, Chap had lost his barn and almost lost the horses. Guilt dug a deeper pit in her gut as she remembered that Dinkum had been hurt.

"I've brought a couple of killers to your ranch. Right now, I have the advantage of knowing that they're here, and can get ahead of them. If you'd take me to a place where I can catch a bus, I'd be grateful."

"And where would you go?"

"Somewhere else."

"Not much of a plan," he observed mildly.

No, it wasn't. But it was all she had.

"Do you honestly think you'd be safer on your own than at the ranch with me and the men?" he asked.

"No. But, like I said, I can't put you and the men in danger." For Hailey, that said it all. Chap and his men had been kind to her; she wouldn't repay them by bringing trouble to their door.

"Lawson and his men want you running scared. If you go off on your own, you'll be playing right into their hands." The look in his eyes was one of challenge. "You're smarter than that. At least, I think you are."

He was right, of course, at least about playing into Doug's hands. About being smart… she wasn't so certain. If she had been smart, she'd have seen through him from the start, but she'd allowed herself to be blinded.

"What do I do?" The words were directed to herself rather than to Chap.

Why was it that the bad guys got to dictate how others lived? Why did *she* have to be the one who lived in fear?

"We'll figure it out. Together."

Together.

He seemed unaware of the effect the last word had upon her, unaware that she had grasped it and now held it to her heart.

"Thank you." Before he could object to her thanking him, she held up a hand. "I know. You don't like to be thanked. But I couldn't help myself."

"You'll be safe enough if you stay inside. There's not a man on this ranch who'd let anyone get to you."

She did her best to blink back tears. "Thank you."

"What did I say about thanking me?"

"Maybe if you'll quit doing kind things, I wouldn't have to."

The warmth in his gaze unsettled her in ways she'd never experienced with Doug. She could scarcely recall why she'd thought she'd loved him in the first place. She'd been in love with being in love. Nothing more.

The realization was a much-needed reminder that she couldn't allow her feelings to spin out of control. Not for Chap. Not for any man. Especially not after her experience with Doug. With an unwavering sense of honor and duty, Chap had nothing in common with her ex-fiancé, but he was dangerous to her in a far different way.

"I won't let anything happen to you," he said. "Until you're ready to face Lawson, you can stay right here."

"I can't stay here forever."

"You won't. When the time is right, you'll do what has to be done."

"How will I know when the time is right?"

"You'll know. You're not alone."

He was correct. She had Chap and his men on her side. More importantly, she had the Lord.

No. She wasn't alone.

Chap kept his anger inside. Not at Hailey, but at the man who continued to terrorize her.

No wonder Lawson wanted her dead. Her testimony could put him away for life. Chap knew he needed to get her to the right people. After weighing the pros and cons of contacting friends from the marshals or colleagues from S&J, he decided to call Josh Harvath again and ask for help. Though the marshals had unmatched resources, he couldn't forget the scandal of a year ago when three marshals had been proven guilty of corruption and murder.

"Hey, buddy," Josh said. "I don't hear from you in months and now I get two calls in a matter of days. What's up?"

Chap filled him in on what had been going on.

Josh gave a low whistle. "You should have said so in the first place. What do you need?"

"Can you assign someone to track Lawson's movements for the next week? I know it's a big ask, but I need to know where he is and what he's doing. Especially if there's a change in his routine."

"Can do." Josh paused. "You doing better?"

Chap thought it over. "Yeah." Despite the danger he and Hailey faced, he felt better than he had in months. Protecting Hailey had given him a purpose, something that had been lacking in his life lately.

"I'll get back to you when I hear anything."

"Thanks, Josh."

His mind more settled now that he'd done something concrete, Chap turned his thoughts to helping Hailey understand that she wasn't alone. She needed time to heal and to feel safe.

When he had been in the SEALs, he and a buddy had decided that they were sheepdogs, protecting sheep from the wolves that preyed on them. Wolves could appear in any form, whether it be foreign terrorists or home-grown ones. Lawson was of the latter variety and was all the more dangerous because of his outward façade of respectability.

Wolves attacked when the sheep were the most vulnerable. And though most people didn't like being compared to sheep, they remained largely unaware of the dangers surrounding them.

In his office, Chap withdrew a Beretta Nano from his gun safe. He routinely carried a Glock as his primary weapon. When he was working a case for S&J, he kept the Beretta holstered at his ankle. Having a second weapon had saved his life on more than one occasion.

Now felt like the right time to bring out the Beretta.

As he strapped the semiautomatic pistol in the holster at his ankle, Dinkum wandered in. "I was wondering when you were going to bring out that bad boy," he said.

"It felt right."

"I'm carrying, too." Dinkum patted the SIG-Sauer at his hip. Though it wasn't unusual to see him armed, neither was it a regular oc-currence.

"Good. We can't be too prepared."

"We gotta talk."

The tone of Dinkum's voice alerted Chap that something was wrong. Seriously wrong.

"What is it?"

Dinkum pointed to the computer. "Can I?"

Chap gestured for his friend to sit. "Have at it."

Dinkum tapped a few keys and brought up an email sent to the ranch account from an un-known sender.

Chap read it aloud,"The barn fire was just the beginning. We're going to keep coming for the woman until we have her. Turn her over to us and save yourself a boatload of trouble." His anger had grown with every word.

"What are you gonna do?" Dinkum asked. "Are you gonna tell Hailey?"

Chap didn't want to tell her, but he didn't have the right to keep this from her.

"I have to."

Dinkum nodded, the lines in his face deeper than usual. "Yeah. That's what I figured."

"Might as well get it over with."

"Want me to go with you?"

"Thanks, but it's something I have to do myself."

Chap found Hailey in the bunkhouse kitchen, singing "Silent Night" in an off-key voice. Somehow, her less-than-perfect voice made the song more engaging, and he paused a moment to listen.

"Hi," he said after she ended one song and before she started another.

She looked up and smiled. "I'm sorry you had to hear that." Her laugh was refreshingly free of self-consciousness. "I'm never going to win a Grammy, though someone might pay me *not* to sing."

"It sounded pretty good to me."

"You're the only one who has ever said that."

"The men can't get enough of your cooking."

Twin dimples appeared at either side of her mouth. "They're easily satisfied."

"I think I'd have an outright rebellion on my hands if you ever left." Before getting the last words out, he wanted to snatch them back. They both knew she would have to leave at some point.

Her dimples vanished. "I can't stay here forever. Someday, I have to go back and face Lawson." She wiped the flour off her hands from where she'd been rolling out a pan of cookies. "What's up?"

"Can't I just appreciate your singing?"

"You don't usually come in here in the middle of the day. Especially when I heard you talking this morning about needing to move cattle to a lower section of the ranch."

She was too perceptive. He'd wanted to ease into this, but maybe it was better just to come out with it. So he plunged ahead.

He didn't pretty it up, knowing Hailey would want the straight of it. "An anonymous threat came in an email. It says that the people after you are going to keep coming."

Frowning, she straightened the corners of the already neatly folded towel. "What are you going to do?" She asked the question as though his answer was only of mild interest.

He'd expected more of a reaction. Fear. Shock. Panic. Something. But not this matter-of-fact acceptance. "What do you think I'm going to do? I'm going to ignore it and keep you safe."

"I wouldn't blame you if you wanted me to leave." She trembled once then stiffened, as though gathering her courage around her. "Trouble's coming."

Anger replaced the concern he'd been feeling. After everything, she still thought he'd kick her out? He crossed his arms over his chest and broadened his stance. The gesture was instinctive, the same one he'd used in the SEALs when faced with a seemingly impossible mission.

"I thought we'd settled this."

She nodded. "I know that's not who you are. It's just that you've done so much for me already. I don't want to put you and your men in any more danger."

There was no way he could allow her to face Lawson and his minions alone. She'd be scooped up by one of his men in a day. Probably less. He had to convince her that staying at the ranch was not just for her safety but for that of him and his men as well.

"We'll be in more danger if we have to go chasing after you and fight off Lawson's men. So no more talk about leaving the ranch. Okay?"

"Okay." She bit down on her lip. "Could you give me some self-defense lessons? If…when …his men come after me again, I want to be prepared."

"Good idea."

Chap was grateful he'd convinced Hailey to drop the idea of leaving the ranch, but he knew this wasn't over. He didn't have any answer to the very real menace they faced, so he did the only thing he could and wrapped his arms around her.

But she was right about one thing. Trouble *was* coming.

SIX

Chap loaded the dishwasher that night. "The men sure liked your meatloaf and potatoes," he said.

Hailey smiled. "Like I said before, it's simple fare. As long as I make enough of it, they like everything."

"Don't kid yourself. They eat everything, but they like—make that *love*—your cooking."

He had taken to helping Hailey as she cleaned up after the evening meal. It felt good to share the events of the day, to talk through the problems of running a ranch.

It occurred to him that they were talking as friends did, and though he and Hailey weren't involved in any romantic sense, they were friends. He tested the word and found that it felt good.

He thought of the friends he'd all but shunned in the last year while he'd dealt with his grief over Lori. They'd repeatedly asked him to join them for a hiking trip, a night out at the movies, a Saturday of stock car racing, but he'd turned them all down. Maybe he should reconsider accepting a few of those invitations.

Whatever the reason, it was time he moved past Lori's death and, though he'd never forget her, join the land of the living again. What accounted for his change of heart? Was it time spent with his pretty stowaway?

While she was otherwise occupied, he studied her, noting the delicacy of her profile. Despite everything she'd been through, it held a quiet repose. But there was strength there as well. Was that what drew him to her, made him want to spend any extra time with her?

It was more than her cooking that pulled him to the kitchen. It was the woman herself. The idea that he was attracted to her was disturbing. The last thing he needed in his life was a woman, especially one with a troubled past.

He pushed the subject away, unwilling to examine it too closely.

After hanging up a dish towel, Hailey poured two cups of coffee and carried them to the table. He sat across from her, enjoying the view. A speck of flour dotted her chin, but he didn't wipe it away.

He liked it just where it was.

Her eyes were fringed with gold lashes.

She'd left them unadorned by makeup. He liked that, too.

She touched her face. "I must look a wreck. Cooking over a hot stove tends to smear my makeup, so I don't usually wear any." A grimace settled on her pretty mouth. "Doug couldn't stand that. He wanted me to look perfect all the time."

"You don't need to worry what he wants. Not anymore."

"You're right." Her mouth bowed up at that. "I envy your friendship with Dinkum. You seem closer than a lot of brothers."

"We are... Do you have any special friends?"

"Not really. Not anymore. When I started dating Doug, I spent more and more time with him. He didn't like me being friends with street people." She frowned. "Thinking back, he didn't like me being friends with anyone. It's all so clear now. He isolated me. Why didn't I see that?" The question was asked more to herself than to him. "There's no one that could be used against you?"

She looked at him curiously. "Why all the questions about my friends?"

Chap wondered if he should share his worries with her. "You said you didn't have any family. Lawson might go after your friends."

Her forehead pleated in a frown. "He doesn't know their names."

He wanted to believe that her friends were safe, but a man like Lawson had ways of tracking down people.

"You're too good for the likes of Lawson."

"It's funny. He always told me that he was too good for me." Her lips pursed. "He never said it aloud, but he let me know it in a thousand ways. I guess I was so flattered by his attention that I didn't realize that he was putting me down every opportunity he had. I think it made him feel good."

"Some people are like that. They have so little going for them that the only way they can feel good about themselves is to hurt others."

"You described Doug to a T. The only thing good to come out of all of this is that I saw him for what he was before we got married."

"You would have seen through him. You're too smart not to pick up on what a phony he is."

"Not to mention a murderer," she added wryly.

"Yeah. Not to mention that."

"Sometimes I'm afraid I'll always be looking over my shoulder, waiting for Doug or one of his men to appear."

Chap reached for her hand, liking the way it fit inside his own. "What did I tell you? We're in this together." He looked down at their linked hands. *What was he thinking?* Had he so easily forgotten the misery that had cloaked him like a shroud after Lori's death? He had no intention of risking his heart again.

The stakes were too high,

Gently, he disengaged his hand. He wouldn't be going down that path. Not with Hailey. Not with any woman.

Getting up early—"hard dark," Chap called it—appealed to her. Working before the men got up gave her the quiet to collect her thoughts, to plan her menus, to pray. And to plan her next steps.

Though she'd tried to downplay her worry after her conversation with Chap about the threatening message, a spurt of fear would occasionally catch her unaware and send tremors up her spine.

The knowledge that Doug and his men were still coming after her—and knew where to find her—was sobering.

What was she supposed to do about it? She wasn't a brave person, but life on the streets had taught her one thing. Take one day at a time. Get through it and then get through the next. And the one after that.

There had been nights after leaving foster

care when she'd shivered herself to sleep in a store doorway with only a sheet of cardboard as cover and had woken to a hunger so intense that her stomach didn't just grumble, it howled in protest. She'd fought off thieves intent on taking her few possessions and had done the same with those intent on recruiting her to gangs. Somehow, she'd gotten through by sheer will and the Lord's grace.

That was what she resolved to do today. She hadn't broken then; she wouldn't break now. After prayer, work was her best defense.

She had breakfast to cook, a kitchen to clean, dinner to prepare and, after that, supper. She would do those things today and do them again tomorrow. And be grateful that she had honest work to earn her keep.

As long as she was doing, worry wouldn't defeat her. Neither would Douglas Lawson and his henchmen.

For the last eight years, she'd earned her living with her catering. Her interest in cooking had started in a foster home. The mother had let Hailey hang around the kitchen. Eventually, she'd turned over most of the cooking to her.

Whether in a down-and-out diner, a glitzy penthouse catering an event for a society matron, or now in an enormous bunkhouse for twelve large men, she was making her cooking work for her. She found satisfaction and, yes, pride in the work. The chopping, mixing, and baking had a kind of rhythm that both soothed and energized her.

Cooking for a group of big, always-hungry men challenged her, made her rethink the recipes she would normally use, simplifying the list of ingredients and baking in huge batches.

The men's appreciation was all the encouragement she needed. It was far better than the picky questions the *ladies who lunch crowd* typically asked when she catered a society affair. Questions like "How many calories does this have in it? I'm dieting to fit in a new dress." Or, "Are you sure you made this with organic flour? My health is so delicate, don't you know?"

With the men, the only question was "Did you make enough?" followed by lip-smacking sounds that let her know they liked what she'd served them. She stirred up another huge bowl of eggs and then ladled them onto the griddle for scrambling. Making eggs-in-a-hole, which she'd wanted to do, took time, and the men were still hungry.

When Dinkum came in for a look-see, as he called it, she smiled at him. "Have you been at the ranch long?"

"Chap and I knew each other when we were

on the Teams. SEALs," he explained upon seeing her blank look. "When he bought this place, he asked me to come ramrod for him. I manage the ranch when he's not here and keep him in line when he is." He chuckled. "I brought my ma along with me. She worked here as cook until she couldn't do it anymore. She passed a year ago."

"I'm sorry." And she was. She didn't remember her own mother and envied the love he'd clearly felt for his own.

"She had a good life. At the end, the boss took care of her like she was his own. Those last days, he'd come sit with her so that I could grab a few hours' sleep. I'd come back and find him holding her hand, like she was his own ma."

Something else to file away about Michael Chapman. He had a soft heart and did right by his men and their families.

When the men filed in for breakfast, they greeted her with jokes and smile. They treated her like a kid sister. She liked the camaraderie and easy teasing that went on around her.

Klaverly continued to make her feel uneasy, with the eyes of a hawk stalking his prey. Watching. Always watching. For what, she didn't know, but she was certain she wouldn't like it.

His face was a map of sharp lines and harsh angles. There was a cruel guise to him that made her think of a boy in one of the foster homes who'd liked to pull the wings off butterflies. He looked like someone who had stared at life and life had stared back, neither one of them pleased with what they'd seen.

She made a point of returning Klaverly's hard stare with one of her own.

Today, she felt the weight of his gaze as it searched her face, his eyes crawling over her like dozens of ants. Though she tried to convince herself that she was imagining things, the cold air that shivered over her in his presence was most definitely real.

Dinkum followed her eyes. "Don't pay Klaverly no mind. Sometimes the mean in a person runs real deep. He was rode hard and put away wet when he was a boy is my guess."

Though she wasn't familiar with the expression, she grasped its meaning and nodded her understanding, experiencing a pang of sympathy for the boy the man had been. She'd run across kids first in the foster system and then on the streets who'd had the same angry look in their eyes.

A commotion erupted in the dining area, and Hailey looked up to see what was going on. Sam had wandered into the room. The big shepherd was a favorite among the men, and not just because he belonged to the boss.

Klaverly jumped up, knocking over his chair as he did so and nearly kicking Sam in the process. "Keep him away from me."

Dinkum crossed the room and hunkered over Sam, smoothing the raised hair at the dog's hackles. "It's all right, boy." He then stood and faced Klaverly. "What do you have against Sam?"

"I don't like mutts. Always slinking around. Looking like they're gonna take a bite out of you."

"Sam wouldn't hurt anyone who didn't need hurting," Dinkum said, earning a scowl from the other man. "He's a decorated soldier. Can you say the same?" When Klaverly didn't answer, Dinkum nodded. "I didn't think so."

"Doesn't matter if I was some pretend soldier like that mongrel. I got a right to eat my breakfast in peace without this mutt bothering me." Klaverly sent a blistering glare Dinkum's way.

He returned the ranch hand's glare with one of his own. "You want to keep in good with the boss? Don't let him hear you bad-mouthing Sam. He and Sam were partners, and he sets a right store by him."

Klaverly stalked out, without picking up his

chair or taking his dishes to the kitchen as the men were accustomed to doing.

Hailey shivered at the animosity in his eyes as he passed her on the way out. There was no reason for him to dislike her, at least none that she could think of.

With Sam at his side, Dinkum crossed the room and wrapped an arm around her shoulders. "Me and the boys won't let him get near you," he promised. "A sweet little girl like you doesn't belong around a no-account like Klaverly."

Sam woofed in what she took as support.

She gave the foreman a grateful smile and pressed his arm with both hands. "Thank you. You're a good friend."

He blushed so sweetly that she kissed his cheek.

Cheers sounded through the room. Dinkum gave an abashed smile that caused her heart to melt. When he enveloped her in a gentle hug, it was as warm as woodsmoke.

She knelt to give Sam a hug, as well, touched when he nuzzled her face.

After setting the kitchen to rights, she headed to the barn. She liked being around the horses and, when Chap or one of the men could accompany her, she frequently made a quick trip to the temporary barn to give them a carrot or an apple. Chap had introduced her to each of the horses, and she'd quickly learned their names.

Nobody was around to go with her today, but she couldn't stand being cooped up inside for another minute. As lovely as the ranch house was, it was beginning to feel like a prison. She bundled up and ventured outside, despite the temperature taking a nosedive. It was now below zero, but the sun had come out, bouncing off the snow and back up to a sky the color of bluebells.

Though the cold was pitiless, the scenery more than made up for it. In the distance, mountains speared upward. Snow-covered pines looked straight from a Christmas card.

Inside the barn, the air was redolent with the aroma of horses and clean hay. She breathed in deeply, enjoying the earthy smells.

Sam trailed her into the barn. He had taken to following her around when he wasn't with Chap, a fact that pleased her immensely. She was surprised to see Klaverly there. Was this where he'd gone after storming out of the dining hall? She thought about leaving but changed her mind. Why should she allow him to deny her a few moments of pleasure with the horses? She did her best to keep her distance and hoped he'd do the same.

She walked over to a stall housing a dainty mare named Gemma and gave her an apple. The mare chomped on it then swallowed with a snort of satisfaction.

"Ma'am," Klaverly said in a diffident voice, "could you hold Billy's head while I use a pick on his hooves?" He gestured to a high-stepping gelding. "He tends to be a bit skittish."

Klaverly talked soothingly to Billy, and though she was still uncomfortable to be so close to him, her heart softened toward the man.

They did their parts companionably, and she wondered if she had misjudged him. Surely no one who could talk so gently to a horse could be all bad. Perhaps he'd only been having a bad moment when he'd snapped at Sam.

He moved to work on Billy's front right hoof. She bent her head to nuzzle the gelding's sleek neck. Before she knew what was happening, Klaverly grabbed her from behind and held the sharp instrument to her throat. "I'll slit your throat if you make a sound."

Unaccustomed to the violence happening in front of him, Billy tossed his big head and gave a loud whinny of distress.

Sam had remained mostly out of sight, but, at that moment he attacked, biting down on Klaverly's arm with his huge jaws.

"Get him off me," the man cried.

Afraid that he would use the pick on Sam, Hailey called to him. "Sam, let go," she said, but the shepherd refused to relinquish his hold.

Blood oozed from Klaverly's arm.

When he managed to pull a knife from his boot, she tried to wrestle it from him, but he flung her away then poised the knife at Sam's throat. With one arm still in the dog's powerful jaws, he wasn't able to slice his throat but got his side instead. With a disgusted sound, he tossed the shepherd to the ground.

Hailey picked herself up, ran to Sam, and knelt over him. "It's all right," she murmured. "You'll be all right."

Sam only whimpered. The pitiful sound tore at her heart.

She got to her feet and beat against Klaverly's chest. "How could you do that? He was only trying to protect me."

He knocked her away easily. "Try that again and I'll gut you like I did him. Help me move him to an empty stall. I don't want him discovered right away. Chapman'll be after me soon enough as it is."

"I have to stop the bleeding."

"Do what I said or I'll finish him off." Klaverly wielded the knife menacingly.

Seeing no way out, she did as he said, the

two of them lifting the dog and carrying him to an unused stall. She found a blanket in the barn and pressed it against the wound on Sam's side.

"No one will see him there," she protested, tears stinging her eyes. "He'll die if he doesn't get help."

"He'll die for sure if you don't do what I say. Now get over here."

Too afraid for Sam's sake to resist, Hailey allowed Klaverly to lead her out of the barn to a pickup parked at the side.

Chap had assigned extra men to guard the ranch, but they were looking for threats from the outside, not from one of their own.

She looked wildly about for help, but the ranch yard was empty. She recalled that Chap had taken a couple of men to take care of the wolves that had come down from the high country to pick off stray cattle.

"I don't want to leave you," he'd said. "Maybe I can send Dinkum with the men and stay here."

But she'd sensed his concern about his stock. He was already doing more for her than she'd ever thought to ask. She couldn't demand that he stay with her.

"Go," she'd said. "I'll be fine. You've got guards posted. No one's going to get to me here."

Klaverly must have guessed at her thoughts. "One word and I'll shoot anyone who tries to help you," he said. "I've got a .45 at my waist." He shoved her into the truck and slammed the door, barely missing her hand as she tried to push against it.

She was trapped.

Where was he taking her?

The sky, which had been clear when she'd gone to the barn only a short while earlier, had darkened to gunmetal gray, the clouds ominous and menacing. Snow fell in random patches as though the clouds were squeezing out a few forgotten flakes. That quickly changed as the light sprinkle turned into a steady fall of white and then morphed into a raging blizzard, snow swirling through the air, making visibility next to impossible.

The storm didn't stop Klaverly, who kept driving, leaning forward to squint out the windshield as though by staring hard enough he could make the snow disappear. Could she grab the gun he'd stuck in his pocket? And what then? Hold it on him and order him to turn back?

It would be child's play for him to take it from her, maybe even pistol-whip her with it. In the meantime, the truck would probably go off the road, leaving them stranded.

She noticed that he favored the arm where Sam had bitten him.

"Wish I'd killed that stupid animal."

Hailey didn't respond, knowing anything she said in Sam's defense would only set off the man again.

When the squall of wind worsened, sending the snow into a whirling tempest of white, she prayed he would have the sense to turn back. Though she hadn't been in the area long, she knew enough to understand that the storm was likely to get worse before it got better.

"We can't keep going," she said.

Klaverly muttered something under his breath but didn't snap at her.

Was he rethinking his plan? A sliver of hope gave her the courage to ask, "Are you turning back to the ranch?"

He made a scoffing sound. "You're kidding, right? After what I did to Chapman's mutt, he'll kill me for sure. Besides, he's got feelings for you. I see it whenever he looks your way. He won't take it lightly that I took you."

She didn't respond to Klaverly's assertion that Chap had feelings for her. She knew he cared about her, just as he cared about anyone needing his help.

Nothing more.

Hailey's shoulders slumped along with her

spirits when her captor refused to turn back. Sick at heart about Sam and worried that she'd be turned over to Lawson, she wondered how long she could hold on.

The answer came swiftly. As long as she had to. "What are you going to do?"

"There's a shack not far away. Ranch hands use it for shelter when a storm kicks up. We'll ride out the storm there."

They had been driving for close to an hour, not nearly long enough to cover the length of Chap's ranch, but still long enough to put a good distance between them and the ranch house.

That faint ray of hope took shape again. Though she hated the idea of being alone with Klaverly, she recognized that holing up in a cabin on Chap's property could make it easier for him to find her. She didn't doubt that he'd be looking for her once he discovered she was missing.

Her captor scowled at her, as though she was to blame for the sudden change in the weather, and switched directions.

She didn't say anything, only kept her gaze fixed on the road ahead. It was nearly impossible to identify landmarks, but she wanted to get a sense of where they were going. If Chap couldn't find her and she had to make her way out of here on her own, she needed to know from which direction they had come.

When the truck pulled to a stop, she braced herself. As much as she didn't want to be caught in a blizzard, she didn't want to be trapped with Klaverly. Though he hadn't said anything, she knew he was scared. It didn't take much to understand why. He'd stabbed Chap's beloved dog and knew he would come after him like fury. Not to mention that he'd kidnapped her.

Frightened men tended to turn mean, and Klaverly didn't need any help in that department.

He let himself out, rounded the truck and yanked her out by her arm. He then grabbed a fistful of hair and half pushed, half dragged her to the cabin.

The expression in his eyes was one of cruel intent. She'd seen that same callousness on the streets. Most of the people she'd met had been kindhearted and generous even though they'd had little, wanting to help another in need, but a few had taken pleasure in hurting anyone who got in their path.

"Chap will kill you if you touch me." She attempted to pull away from him, but Klaverly only tightened his hold on her hair until she cried out in pain. "He'll catch you. You have to know that."

"He couldn't catch a cold if he was standing in four feet of snow." But the sweat that sheened his forehead belied his words, and she knew he was afraid of Chap.

Seconds later, his bravado was back in full force. "No one's gonna find you. Not here. Not anywhere."

"I suppose that means you intend on killing me?"

"No way. You're worth a hundred grand."

Had Doug offered the man money? She tried bluffing. "I don't have any family to pay a ransom."

"Don't play dumb with me. The night of the fire, when those two men tried to kidnap you, I knew you were important to someone. I nosed around town, asked some questions." He stroked his jaw. "They sussed me out and offered me a whole lot of dough if I brought you to them."

His eyes took on a considering expression. "Maybe I'll hold out for more," he said, his mouth stretching in a grin so full of greed that she longed to slap it from his face.

Some of what she felt must have showed in her eyes. He cackled. "Don't even be thinking of hittin' me, 'cause I hit back. You being a woman don't change that."

"You're a real gentleman." She didn't bother hiding her loathing for him.

"Careful, sweetheart." He pulled a disgusting-looking kerchief from his pocket and she almost gagged just looking at it. "You keep up with your smart-mouthing, and I may stuff this into that pretty face of yours." The malice in his voice sent frissons of fear dancing along her spine.

She remained silent after that, unable to stomach the thought of the rag being stuffed in her mouth. Klaverly was just the type to use such a tactic to break her spirit.

In the meantime, it was up to her to help herself. She wasn't helpless. Not by a long shot. She'd find a way out of this.

He scratched his head. "I don't know what you did to the dude that wants you back so much he's willing to shell out a hundred grand for you, but if he's got that much money, you should've made nice with him."

"Money isn't everything," she said quietly. Klaverly grinned once more. "Only a few more hours and you'll be on your way." He gave a nasty laugh.

She needed to escape. Or be sold to Doug.

Klaverly put a big hand on her shoulder and spun her around. "Just to make sure you don't act up," he said and bound her hands together.

He seemed to take pleasure in tying the rope as tightly as possible, the rough hemp biting into her skin.

He then pushed her into a corner. "Mind your manners, and we'll get along just fine." He laughed at his own words, as if he'd said something particularly clever.

Hailey kept her head down. She'd mind her manners, all right. She'd mind them until she found an opening, and then she'd do her best to make him mind his own.

Chap looked for Hailey in the bunkhouse kitchen. Not finding her there, he went to the main house.

"Have you seen Hailey?" he asked the house-keeper.

"No, sir. Not since she went to the barn with a basket of apples and carrots." They'd moved the horses to the old barn, one he hadn't gotten around to tearing down when the more recent one had been built. Now he was grateful he hadn't as it made a temporary shelter for the animals. "I thought I'd told her to stay inside."

"She was concerned about the horses in their new quarters and wanted to give them a treat."

Despite his annoyance with Hailey, he couldn't help smiling. She had taken a liking to the horses and occasionally slipped away to give them treats. With the guards he'd posted, she ought to be safe enough. Still, he'd talk with her and emphasize that she needed to stay in the house or the bunkhouse.

He grabbed a thermos of hot chocolate to take along with him, thinking they could share it and feed the animals together.

Ordinarily, he wouldn't be spending time in the middle of the day feeding horses, but the idea of spending time with Hailey was undeniably appealing.

When he looked in the barn, he didn't find her. He started a more thorough search when a faint whimper from a stall had him heading in that direction. There, he found, not Hailey, but Sam huddled in a corner in a puddle of blood.

Chap removed the blanket from Sam's side and gently probed the wound. He had been stabbed. Fury such as he'd never known rolled through him at the sight. He clamped down on it so that he could tend to the shepherd.

"It'll be all right, boy," he murmured.

It didn't look like the knife had hit any vital organs, but the wound was deep enough. "We'll get you help." He crossed the aisle to the first-aid kit he kept in the barn and returned with gauze, bandages and alcohol swabs.

Tenderly, he cleaned the wound and applied the bandage.

Dinkum stepped in at that moment. "Boss, have you seen Hailey? I haven't seen—" He noticed Sam. "What happened?"

"He's been knifed."

Why would anyone stab his dog? It made no sense…unless Sam had been defending someone from an attack and the attacker had reacted by stabbing him.

His thoughts ground to a halt as he felt a tick in his blood. "What were you saying about Hailey?"

"No one can find her. It's past dinnertime, and she's never late with meals. I got worried and came looking for her. The men are ready to stage a mutiny." Dinkum, too, knelt beside Sam. "Is it bad?"

"Bad enough."

Dinkum's face scrunched in a frown. "One of the hands told me he saw Klaverly take off in a pickup and that it looked like he had someone with him. I couldn't figure it out since I hadn't given him a job that needed a truck."

Chap didn't like how the pieces were stacking up. Worry over Sam warred with concern for her. If Klaverly had taken her…

With infinite care, Chap lifted Sam and carried him to a truck. He found a blanket in the back seat and tucked it around him. "Take him to the vet and stay with him." He clapped a hand on his friend's shoulder and squeezed. "You know what Sam means to me."

"Same as he does to me." Though Dinkum's eyes were hard, his voice turned soft. "I'll do my best by him."

"I know you will. Thanks, man. I owe you."

"You don't owe me a thing," Dinkum said and slid into the driver's seat. He started up the engine and then paused. "And it won't hurt my feelings none if you do to Klaverly what he did to Sam. Now go get our girl and bring her home."

Chap didn't say what they were both thinking.

He might already be too late.

SEVEN

Hailey did her best to keep Klaverly from seeing how truly scared she was—men like him fed on the fear of others—but the look in his eyes was enough to have her scooting as far back in the corner of the cabin as possible. His leer told her that he knew exactly what she was doing and was amused by it.

"Don't worry, honey," he said, the word causing her to cringe. "My instructions said you weren't to be harmed. If you are, no money. And as pretty as you are, I ain't passing up a hundred thousand dollars for the likes of you."

She supposed she should be grateful to Doug for that, but she was having a hard time working up any gratitude to the man who had set the whole thing in motion.

She tried to appeal to her captor's sense of self-preservation. "You know what Chap will do to you when he finds you. There's nowhere you can hide. Nowhere you'll be safe. Leave me here and take off. You can get a head start on him. You'll be out of the state before he knows what happened." She slid him a knowing look. "Isn't that what you want? To show him up?"

Klaverly looked tempted but then shook his head. "I can't outrun him in this storm."

"How do you know? He doesn't know where we are. Take off now, and he'll never find you."

"How come you're so interested in my welfare all of a sudden?"

Hailey knew she couldn't convince him that it was out of concern for him, and so she went with the truth. "To save my own skin," she said bluntly. "You leave me here, and eventually someone will find me, meaning I won't get sold to some lowlife. We both win."

"And I won't get the hundred grand you'll bring if I turn you over."

"But you won't have to face Chap. You're afraid of him. I can tell." Instantly, she knew she'd said the wrong thing. The man's ego wouldn't allow it to stand. Klaverly was one of those men who had to appear the best at anything he did. Very much like Doug. They were two of a kind, egotistical and ruthless.

Klaverly made a move toward her, hand raised, ready to strike, but at the last minute he held back and sneered. "I thought about that, but I can handle him. He thinks he's a big-shot because he was a US marshal and a SEAL once upon a time, but that was years ago. He's over-the-hill now." He chuckled.

"I'll settle for making a hundred large," he said and then smirked. "A hundred thou will set me up good. Real good." He all but smacked his lips. "I ain't never had nothin' good in my life. Always workin' penny-ante jobs that don't pay squat. Like being a ranch hand. Now's my turn, and I aim on takin' it."

Hailey sank back. So much for that tactic. But she wasn't giving up.

He took off his coat and cranked his head to look at his arm. "That dog near took off my arm."

She refrained from saying *good*. "Dog bites can be dangerous. You ought to have that looked at."

"It's nothin' a little antiseptic won't handle."

She made a point of looking around. "And where're you going to get that?"

"Why don't you mind your own business?"

"That's what I'm doing. If something happens to you, I'm all alone with no way to get help."

His face took on a thoughtful expression.

Maybe if she could convince him to get help, she'd find an opportunity to escape.

"You don't know what you're talking about. My arm's fine."

She was tempted to ask if this was the same arm he'd said that Sam nearly took off but thought better of it.

"The rope around my wrists is really tight. Could you loosen it?" She gritted her teeth. "Please." She ground out the word, though it grated on her to beg him for anything, even a little human decency.

"How stupid do you think I am? Batting those big green eyes at me isn't going to get you anything, so you might as well sit back and make yourself comfortable." The cruelty in his eyes echoed the hateful words. He knew she wasn't going to get comfortable, not with her hands tied behind her back.

"You must have been hurt badly as a child," she said quietly, recalling what Dinkum had said about him.

"What're you talking about?" The sharpness of his voice told her that she'd hit a nerve.

"Just that cruelty like yours doesn't come from nowhere. Someone must have hurt you to make you want to do the same to others. I'm sorry for you," she added.

"I don't need nobody to feel sorry for me." But the words sounded defensive rather than angry. "My pa was a Bible-thumping hypocrite, who believed in 'spare the rod and spoil the child.'" He threw her a resentful look. "What are you, anyway? Some kind of shrink? No one hurt me. I'm just fine. More than fine. So mind your own business and quit messing in mine."

"If that's what you want."

"What do you know about what I want? The only reason I'm bothering with you is that you're worth a whole bunch of money." The defensiveness had vanished. "Best you keep your mouth shut or I'll stick a rag in it and shut it for you."

The anger was back, and she did as she was told, but she couldn't help wondering what had turned the child he'd been into the man he'd become. For a fraction of a second, she felt something akin to pity for him.

But she couldn't afford to waste energy feeling sorry for the man. She'd had one opportunity to convince him to let her go, and she'd blown it. Right now, she didn't have any options but to wait. That didn't mean she was giving up, though. Far from it.

She knew Chap would come for her. Her job was to hold on until he got there. She felt a nail protruding from the rough wall at her back. Could she use it to saw through the ropes until they gave way?

Trying to keep her movements subtle, she rubbed her rope-bound wrists back and forth over the nail.

Did she feel the ropes loosening?

It was painstaking work, and every time she sawed back and forth, she felt blood trickle down her hands, but she kept at it. Ignoring the pain. Ignoring the panic. The coppery smell of blood filled her nostrils, and she wondered if her captor could smell it, too.

It couldn't be helped.

After what seemed hours of struggling, though it was probably less than twenty minutes, she gave one final swipe of her bound wrists against the nail, roughing up the ropes enough to wriggle her hands free. She kept her arms in place, not wanting to let Klaverly know she was free. Her hands and fingers tingled like hundreds of bee stings as her circulation returned, and she gave herself a few minutes before she made her move.

She'd have only one opportunity to take him out. That meant she had to watch for the right moment.

When he turned his back to her to look out the window, she sprang. She'd already identified a poker near the fireplace to use, grabbed for it and swung it with all her might, aiming for the back of his head. However, he turned too soon and the poker caught him on his upper arm instead. That wasn't all bad, though, as it hit directly on the dog bite.

He howled in anger, grasping his wounded arm. "You made a big mistake there, little gal. And now you're going to pay for it."

She didn't have time to worry over the threat.

He advanced on her with a glower of hate so intense that she nearly withered beneath it, but she couldn't afford to let fear overwhelm her. She had only one choice. *Fight.*

Still armed with the poker, she swung it in a wide arc, aiming for his kidneys, but she'd miscalculated and hit him in the ribs instead. Though the blow had to be painful, it hadn't taken him down.

She swung again, this time aiming for the groin. She hadn't forgotten the .45 he carried. Would he use it on her? She didn't think so. He'd said that he had to bring her in alive. In any case, she had to risk it. If she didn't do anything, she'd be turned over to Doug.

Klaverly bared his teeth when the blow barely missed its target and connected with his upper thigh.

"You ought not to mess with me." The snarl in his voice was almost as terrifying as the vile gleam in his eyes. With one swift motion, he grabbed the poker from her.

She bemoaned the loss of her weapon, but she wouldn't let that stop her. She ducked his swipes with it, then pivoted on her left foot and, striking out with her right leg, caught him in the abdomen.

He grunted out his pain, but she knew he'd be on her again. If one of those ham-sized fists caught her in the jaw, she'd be out. If he succeeded in knocking her to the ground, she'd be totally at his mercy. A kick from one of his boot-clad feet would probably break every rib she had.

She recalled a friend's advice on how to fend off predators. *Keep moving. He can't hurt you if he can't catch you.*

Now, she did her best to do just that, but the small space and her own waning energy were working against her. She fought with everything she had, but he was too big, too strong. Even using the down-and-dirty moves she'd picked up in defending herself on the streets, she couldn't best him.

She recalled a feral cat that'd lived in the alley behind the diner where she'd had her first real job. The cat had played with a mouse until it had grown tired of the game. Then the cat had pounced, and it was game over. That was how she felt now.

Klaverly was only playing with her. When

he grew tired of the sport, he'd pounce and make her hurt.

"Might as well give it up," he told her. "You'll only get hurt more."

He was right. But, not willing to give in, Hailey head-butted him, causing her ears to ring. It was a last-ditch move, probably causing her more pain than it did him, but it was all she had.

He laughed at the pathetic attempt. "That all you got?"

He drew back his fist and knocked her to the ground. Still reeling from the blow, she couldn't get out of the way fast enough when he reared back his leg and, as she'd feared, kicked her in the ribs.

Agony tore through her, and it was all she could do not to cry out in pain. Finally, she curled in the fetal position, trying to block his kicks as best she could.

"You asked for it, lady. Try anything like that again and you'll be sorry." After hauling her to her feet, he picked her up as though she weighed nothing and dumped her into the corner. There, he bound both her hands and her feet.

"I have to give it to you. You put up a good fight given you're so puny." He swiped at the arm she'd struck with the poker, using the kerchief he'd threatened her with earlier.

She hoped he got an infection from it and was gratified when the kerchief came away bloody.

The metallic taste of her own blood filled her mouth; her jaw throbbed and her ribs ached, but she couldn't bring herself to regret fighting back.

Not for a minute.

Chap reined in the instinct to push the truck harder, knowing that would spell disaster on the treacherous roads. The storm had grown teeth, the snow rapidly covering everything in its wake.

No one who had weathered one of Wyoming's winter storms would be out in this one if they could help it, which meant Klaverly, if he had any sense, would be looking for shelter.

Driving in a blizzard was nothing new to Chap and he kept the truck at a steady speed, tapping on the brakes when necessary and turning into slides rather than fighting them while he did his best not to think of what Hailey's kidnapper might be doing to her. No, Klaverly didn't scare Chap, but what he could be doing to Hailey did. Even if Klaverly didn't harm her, turning her over to Douglas Lawson would spell her death warrant. From everything he'd learned about the man, he was ruthless and would eat a snake like Klaverly for dinner and still be hungry for supper.

Images too horrific to contemplate tormented him. The possibility of finding Hailey alive and unharmed was growing dimmer by the moment as the storm brewed and stewed in a nasty mix of snow and wind that showed no sign of letting up. He resented every extra minute he spent in keeping the truck on the road, minutes that prevented him from reaching Hailey sooner.

Prayers he no longer believed in beckoned, but he pushed them away. He didn't have time. It took everything he had to thrust his worry for Hailey and Sam from his mind and concentrate on the road.

The one thing he had going for him was that Klaverly was fairly new to the area and didn't know a lot of places where he could hole up. A dim speck of hope had him pulling to the side of the road and opening up his tablet, where he brought up an aerial view of the ranch.

He zeroed in on the far eastern end of the property. There it was. A cabin. The structure was so far out that it wasn't used much, but a couple of months ago, he'd assigned Klaverly to round up some strays in the area. He may have seen it and remembered it.

Chap put the tablet away and started up

again. It wasn't much, but it was all he had, and he clung to the thread as he would a lifeline.

He encountered a drift of snow so deep it came up to the door handles, but the truck rolled through it with scarcely a grumble. Slow and steady, he reminded himself when the urge to hit the gas threatened to rear its head again.

After forty-five minutes of excruciatingly slow driving, he checked the tablet again. By his calculations, the cabin shouldn't be far.

Until now, he hadn't thought of what he'd do when he reached it. If he failed to find Klaverly and Hailey there, Chap didn't know what he'd do next. He pushed that from his mind and kept going.

Failure is not an option.

When Chap made out a column of smoke puffing from a chimney, he knew he was headed in the right direction. A few minutes later, he came upon the cabin. Not wanting to alert Klaverly of his presence until the last minute, he parked a few yards away and tramped through knee-high snow.

He reminded himself that it might not be Klaverly and Hailey at the cabin, but common sense told him that it was. Who else would be out in a storm like this?

The front door was the only ingress and,

seeing no reason to be subtle at this point, he kicked it open. If it had been in other circumstances, he might have smiled. "Door Kicker" was a favorite nickname for a navy SEAL.

Obviously startled when the door crashed open, Klaverly jumped back. His gaze darted about.

What Chap found inside sent waves of rage roiling through him. Hailey, bound hand and foot, had been shoved into a corner. Red blotches stained her face, probably from crying. There were darkening marks under her eyes and on the crest of her cheekbone. More concerning, though, was the dried blood on her jacket.

What had Klaverly done to her?

"Chap," she cried. "He hurt Sam."

In that instant, he wanted to take her in his arms and hug her. She'd been kidnapped, beaten, and yet her first thought was for the German shepherd.

"I know," he said without taking his gaze from Klaverly. "He's being taken care of."

Rushing an enemy was a fool's move, and he was no fool, but Klaverly didn't give him a choice. When he pulled a .45 from the back of his waistband, Chap was ready and kicked the weapon from his enemy's hand. The feverish glint in his opponent's gaze warned Chap that they were playing for keeps.

Though he was armed, Chap didn't want to use his weapon. In the small space, a bullet could easily ricochet and hit Hailey or him. Also, he wanted Klaverly alive, to question him and find out where he'd gotten his orders.

Chap had top-notch training courtesy of the United States Navy on his side, but his foe had pure meanness. He didn't underestimate it. He'd seen it in action on the battlefield. Meanness gave an edge.

His opponent was already jacked up on adrenaline. The two men were evenly matched in size and strength, and Chap knew he was in for the fight of his life.

When Klaverly came at him, Chap ducked a blow to his head and then went in hard. The slap of flesh against flesh and pain-filled grunt echoing pain-filled grunt packed the small space.

After Chap had gotten in a good crack to Klaverly's jaw, the man extracted a knife from his boot. The same knife he'd used on Sam?

Chap eyed the weapon, a new wave of anger pouring through him. He couldn't afford the luxury of giving in to it, so he focused on the way his opponent was handling the weapon. Clearly, he wasn't an amateur in using the deadly blade.

Klaverly didn't know it, but he'd done Chap

a favor in pulling the knife. It gave him extra impetus to take the man down and see that he paid for what he'd done to Sam and Hailey.

"You won't like what I can do with this," he said. "Especially if I start in on her. I could carve up that pretty face of hers real nice so that no man would ever look at her again."

Chap bridled the anger he'd promised himself he wouldn't give in to. "You're real brave. Using a knife on an animal and threatening a woman with it."

"That dog of yours ought to be put down. Near took my arm off. I did the world a favor by knifing him," Klaverly said, mouth stretching into an ugly sneer. "By the way, how is the mongrel? Is he dead yet?"

Chap didn't react. It didn't take much to understand that the man was trying to get under his skin, thereby causing him to make a mistake. "He's better than you'll be once I finish with you."

Klaverly sliced through the air with the knife, the metal gleaming even in the dim light. "Come and get it. What's the matter?" he taunted when Chap didn't react immediately. "Chicken?"

Chap didn't respond. Rather than going for the knife, as Klaverly no doubt expected, he went in low and grabbed him by the legs, sending them both sprawling to the floor and knocking the knife from his hand.

His enemy brawled like a street fighter, using every dirty trick in the book. They each scrabbled across the floor for the weapon and grappled for possession. When Chap's fingertips brushed the hilt of the knife, he stretched to get a grip on it. He nearly had it, but Klaverly pulled him away, wrapped an arm, thick as a tree branch, around Chap's neck and squeezed.

Chap struggled to breathe, white dots dancing in front of his eyes. Somewhere in the distance, he thought he heard Hailey's voice. The brain shuts down without oxygen, and he knew he was in danger of passing out.

Or worse.

Only the thought that he would leave Hailey to Klaverly's nonexistent mercy kept him conscious.

With herculean effort, he dislodged his enemy's arm and pushed himself out of his reach. Oxygen filled his nostrils. Nothing had ever smelled so sweet, and he inhaled deeply. Another minute, two at the most, and he'd be all right, but he wasn't given a minute. Or even a fraction of one.

Klaverly got to his feet. By the time Chap had done the same, his foe had attacked, breaking through Chap's defensive guard to use his thumbs to try to gouge out his eyes.

Chap threw him off then gripped the man's wrists and forced his arms back, but Klaverly wrenched free and went after the knife again, this time succeeding in grasping it. He closed a hand around it and lashed out with his right arm.

Chap jumped back, but not soon enough. The blade nicked his upper arm. Too intent on fending off his enemy, he didn't register the pain but knew it would come back to bite him soon enough.

His enemy's eyes blazed with satisfaction at having drawn first blood. "You're always strutting around, acting like you're something special because you were a navy SEAL. Looks like you're not so special after all. You're just a has-been. Make that a *never-was*."

Chap didn't give his opponent the satisfaction of an answer. He noticed that Klaverly telegraphed his moves with his feet. It was a small tell but allowed him to know his enemy was going to come at him from the right.

When he attacked, Chap was ready. He shifted his weight and presented his side, making for a smaller target. He dodged what would have been a slash to the ribs by trapping Klaverly's arm, locking up the wrist, and using his own momentum to slam him against the cabin wall.

Klaverly spun around and issued a series of words so foul that Chap cringed, wishing Hailey hadn't been subjected to them. From the blood that spurted down his face, Chap figured the man's nose was broken.

Good.

In his concern for her, he momentarily lost focus, allowing Klaverly to take a swing at Chap, his fist connecting with the side of his head.

With his good arm, Chap struck out with his elbow, ramming it into his attacker's solar plexus. He then torqued his arm up against his back, leveraging his weight against him and making him drop the weapon. With his grip tight on Klaverly's wrist, thereby controlling him, he used his other hand to search the man for more weapons, coming away with a set of brass knuckles.

When Klaverly cried out, Chap eased up on the pressure, but only fractionally.

"You broke it," the man shouted. "You broke my arm."

Chap didn't bother responding. For what the bully had done to Sam and to Hailey, he was tempted to do a lot worse. He threw Klaverly to the floor and fixed him with a hard stare.

"Move and I'll really hurt you. That's a promise." He then turned to Hailey and freed her hands and ankles.

She rubbed her wrists together. His lips tightened as he saw blood trickling down her arms.

While she worked on getting her circulation back, Chap hunkered down and held the brass knuckles in front of Klaverly's face. "Were you planning on using these on her if she didn't cooperate? What kind of man kidnaps a woman and is ready to use brass knuckles on her before turning her over to a man who plans to kill her?"

"It weren't personal," Klaverly muttered. "It was business. Pure and simple. Can't blame a man for wanting to get ahead."

"It looked plenty personal to me." He grabbed the man's arm and yanked him up. "Was it worth it?"

Klaverly snapped, "What are you trying to do? Break it again?"

Chap stared with disgust at the coward. "It's not broken. If it was, I couldn't have pulled you up by it." He turned to Hailey. "Are you all right?"

She brushed that aside. "Never mind about me. What about Sam?"

"Dinkum took him to the vet." He kept his

answer deliberately vague. No sense in saying he, too, was worried about Sam and adding to her fears.

Klaverly spat. "I can't be the only one your man would offer money to," he said to Hailey. "If he wants you back bad enough, he'll pay someone else to come after you like I did." A sly look slid across his face as he focused on Chap. "Maybe you'll turn her in yourself. That kind of money can help you rebuild your barn."

Chap tensed but didn't allow himself to react otherwise. If he did, he might have really broken the man's arm, along with a couple of ribs as well. Could Hailey have thought the same thing? Could she believe that he would turn her over to Lawson?

He didn't respond to the taunt. "We'll see how you like your new accommodations once we get you to jail. You'll be sitting in a cell by night."

Klaverly continued to whine, but Chap didn't pay any attention. After tying his wrists together with the same rope the jerk had used on Hailey, he dragged him to the truck and tossed him in the back. Using bungee cords he routinely kept there, he secured Klaverly to the bed of the truck.

"I'll freeze in here," the man groused.

Chap found a rag and stuffed it in his mouth,

then placed a tarp over him, not to protect him from the elements but to keep him from being seen once they reached town. The fewer questions he had to answer, the better.

That done, he hurried back for Hailey. Her lips were taking on a bluish tint and she was shaking uncontrollably. He knew it wasn't just reaction from the cold; she was suffering from shock as well.

First, though, he needed to know about the blood on her jacket and pointed to it. "What did Klaverly do to you?"

She looked confused and then understanding appeared in her eyes. "The blood? That's Sam's. Klaverly made me help him carry him to a stall where you wouldn't find him right away."

Chap drew her close, and she shivered in his arms.

Needing to get her warmed up, he carried her to the truck. After strapping the seat belt around her, he turned the heater on, tucked a blanket over her, then held the thermos of hot chocolate to her lips. "Take a sip," he urged.

She managed a small sip and closed her eyes.

Away from the dim light of the cabin, he got a better look at the bruises and abrasions marring the delicate skin of her face.

Klaverly would pay for what he'd done. He'd pay big-time.

EIGHT

Hailey didn't talk much on the way to town. She excused herself by claiming she was tired, but the truth was she was scared. Klaverly's actions showed that there would always be desperate men willing to do Lawson's bidding. She wasn't safe here.

Guilt had piled on in a nasty heap as well. She'd brought not just danger to Chap's ranch but real pain when Klaverly had knifed Sam. She knew how much Sam meant to Chap, and though she hadn't set the events in motion, she had been the cause of them.

If Sam died…

She shook her head, unwilling to go there even in her thoughts.

First the fire, and now this. How much more trouble could she bring to the people and the animals she'd learned to care for? She couldn't expect Chap or his men to risk their lives in defending her.

As a child, Hailey had dreamed of a handsome prince who would rescue her from the unloving foster home where she had been placed. One home had been special, where the foster parents had truly cared about the children placed with them, but they had moved to another state. Hailey had begged them to take her with them, but that had been impossible.

So, she had made the best of it and gotten through the worst times by making up stories to entertain herself.

Today, that story had come true, though not in the way she'd imagined it. A prince had rescued her. He hadn't worn a stiffly pressed uniform complete with epaulets. Nor had he carried a gleaming sword and shield. Instead, he'd been dressed in wool and denim and had been armed with courage and integrity.

The reality was so much better than the dream, but that reality also included the prince being wounded. She wanted to tend to those wounds.

But Chap wasn't a prince. What's more, he could never be hers. She couldn't allow herself to fall for him, or any man, like she had for Doug. She'd fallen for what she now knew to be a snake in the grass too easily, and though Chap was nothing like Doug, he still represented danger.

To her heart.

She let out a breath that was clogging her throat. It would be easy to give in to the temptation to lean into him, to absorb his strength and courage, but that wasn't an option.

Hailey knew Chap was caught between concern for her and worry over Sam. For her, there was no choice.

"We're getting you to the hospital," he said.

She shook her head. "First, we see about Sam." She blinked rapidly, an attempt to forestall tears. "If it hadn't been for me—"

"We're not going there," Chap said. "Sam's strong. He'll make it."

"He risked his life to help me."

"And he'd do it again," Chap said. "Sam's a real-life hero. In Afghanistan, he found a wounded soldier pinned down by rubble in a bombed-out building. He alerted me, then went back to stay with the man until some buddies and I could pull him out. He couldn't leave that soldier. Just like he couldn't leave you. It isn't in him."

She sniffled. "Okay. Now you're really going to make me cry."

"Nothing wrong with tears. They show you care." He handed her a handkerchief.

"This is getting to be a habit," she said and blew her nose. "An embarrassing one."

"What Klaverly said about turning you over to Lawson—"

"You don't think I believed that for a second, do you?"

"No." He drew out the word. "Just wanted to make sure."

"You are the most honorable man I know. Klaverly can't imagine anyone behaving honorably because he has no honor of his own."

"Thank you."

"You don't need to thank me. It's the truth."

With those words, she felt her heart turn over. She frowned at the thought. What she was feeling was nothing more than a reaction to what she'd been through, Hailey assured herself. It certainly had nothing to do with the man beside her, whatever her ideas about him being a prince.

Nothing at all.

The trip to town was painstakingly slow. Once they reached it, Chap headed toward the jail. "We'll take out the trash first," he said, hitching his chin toward the truck bed. "Then we'll check on Sam."

The sheriff's office and town jail both resided in a squat brick building, a utilitarian structure that made no bones of being anything other than what it was. Even a coating of fresh snow couldn't hide its unattractive lines and grim purpose.

Chap climbed out of the truck, undid the bungee cords holding Klaverly in place, and hauled him inside. Frost covering the man's face, and frozen on his mustache and beard, couldn't disguise the look of hatred he directed Chap's way. The rag in his mouth kept him from yelling his head off and complaining about his treatment.

With a none-too-gentle shove forward, Chap directed the man toward the jail, opened the door, and gave him one more thrust for good measure.

"Got a customer for you," he told the sheriff.

Victoria Crane's office was empty but for the sheriff herself. She looked up, smiling when she saw Chap. Vic was a fine woman, and pretty along with it, but there was no spark with her. At least not for him. He looked on her as a friend and nothing more.

Her smile turned quizzical when she took in his prisoner.

She eyed Klaverly with interest. "I'm guessing you had your reasons for turning him into a block of ice."

"You're right. I did."

Vic pulled the rag from Klaverly's mouth. "What do you have to say for yourself?"

"I need a doctor," the man whined, glaring at her. "Chapman broke my arm. He oughta be arrested."

The sheriff stared at him without an ounce of compassion.

"What about my arm?" Klaverly demanded. "I need to see a doctor."

Chap had had enough. He didn't try to defend himself to the sheriff, except to say, "He knifed Sam."

Vic had a soft spot for Sam. Chap just hoped she would leave the soft spot she had for him out of it. Especially since he had to bring Hailey in to give her statement.

"I need more to go on before I toss him in a cell," the sheriff said.

Reluctantly, Chap returned to the truck to get Hailey. He hated to make her do this now, when she was still in shock from the cold and Klaverly's manhandling, but it had to be done for the man to be put in jail.

Hailey answered Vic's questions with a minimum of words.

"You'll need to file a real report," the sheriff said.

"Look, can we do it tomorrow?" Chap asked. "Hailey is dead-tired. For that matter, so am I."

A frown worked its way across Vic's mouth, but she nodded. "Sure."

She called one of her deputies to take Klaverly to the cellblock. Cellblock was too grand a name for the three cells that made it up. She then shifted her attention to Chap.

"You don't have to worry about him," she said now, jerking a thumb in Klaverly's direction. "We'll give him our best accommodations. About that statement—"

"We'll come in tomorrow and give it."

"See that you do. And let me know how Sam's doing. I may be calling on you to help pull drivers out of the snowdrifts. City people don't know when to stay off the roads. Think because they have snow tires on their big shiny SUVs that they're good to go." Humor took away the sting of annoyance in her voice.

He grinned. "Don't I know it." It wouldn't be the first time he'd been called to pull a car out of a snowdrift. "I'll be glad to help."

"Thanks."

Chap and Hailey returned to the truck.

Her eyes were fierce. "He didn't have to hurt Sam that way. I hope he goes away a long time for that."

"Same here."

Klaverly's mean ran deep. Chap had encountered other people who were the same, those who liked to inflict pain for the simple reason that they could. He'd met his fair share of such individuals in Afghanistan, but he'd encountered enough of the domestic variety to tell him cruelty knew no nationality or borders.

"Klaverly's going to talk," Chap said reluctantly. "The sheriff will have questions. So far, we've been able to avoid announcing you're staying at the ranch, but it's going to get out. We have to be prepared."

"I know," she said. "But for right now, we have to see to Sam."

Chap's heart did a little flip-flop in his chest. Her first thought wasn't for her own safety but for Sam's well-being.

By the time they reached the vet's office, Chap wished he still believed in prayer. He saw Hailey with her eyes closed and, though her lips weren't moving, he knew she was praying.

Her belief touched a forgotten place within his heart. He'd successfully rooted faith from his life, but talking with Hailey and hearing her fervent belief had stirred memories he preferred to leave in the past.

Unwillingly, he recalled his mother's quiet faith, a faith that had sustained her when his father had been killed in an industrial accident and she'd contracted cancer soon thereafter. He'd held on to his own faith, through the deaths of his parents, even during the horrors of war, but it had died along with Lori. What kind of God allowed an innocent woman to be gunned down?

Despite all Hailey had been through, she never questioned that God loved her, that He was in charge. For a fraction of a moment, he was envious of her belief, her unshakable faith, but that instant passed and he banished the envy he had entertained.

He turned to look at her. With the abrasions on her face and blood on her coat, she was bound to attract attention. That was the last thing they wanted. "You don't have to come in," he said. "I'll leave the engine on, the heater going."

"I'm not letting you face this alone. We'll figure this out together," she said, repeating the words he'd told her a few days ago.

When they stepped inside the vet's office, the wind rushed in along with them.

Dinkum spotted them and made his way over. "No news yet."

They took seats and prepared to wait. Fortunately, there was only one other person waiting.

Ten minutes later, the vet, a red-haired woman who had taken care of Chap's animals since he'd started up the ranch, appeared.

He swallowed hard, feeling that his own life was at stake. "Doc?"

The lady's expression was forbidding. "Whoever did that to that beautiful animal should be…." She shook her head. "Not my place. Sam's going to pull through. He might not have made it if someone hadn't had the forethought to stop the bleeding in the first place."

Hailey. She had saved Sam's life with that act of compassion. He shook the doctor's hand. "Thank you." He didn't know what else to say and searched awkwardly for something.

"You might try thanking God. Doctors are limited in what we can do. Sometimes we need help from the Master Healer."

He felt the weight of Hailey's gaze on him. "Thank you, again, Doctor. Can I see him?"

"You can see him, but only for a minute. He's sedated right now and will probably sleep for the next eight hours. I suggest you get some sleep yourselves—you're all looking a little worse for wear—and then come back in the morning." Her gaze rested on Hailey's face and coat. "Anything I need to report to the police here?"

"It's being taken care of," Sam said. "My… friend…was beaten up trying to protect Sam. The man who did it is in jail."

"That's good enough for me."

Though Chap wanted to stay with Sam, he

recognized the wisdom of her advice in getting some rest.

A nurse led him to a room where Sam lay on a paper sheet atop a large table.

A lump lodged in Chap's throat at the sight. Sam had come through two tours of duty and had been his partner in the marshals for over ten years, only to be wounded and almost killed by a greedy two-bit wannabe of a cowboy.

Tenderly, he stroked the shepherd's head. "You were a hero today, boy. I'll never forget it."

After another few minutes, Chap returned to the waiting room to see Hailey leaning against Dinkum's shoulder, her face gray with exhaustion.

When she saw him, she jumped up. "How is he?"

"Sleeping. But he's going to be all right." The vet had said the same thing, but he'd had to see for himself. "I'll check in tomorrow. In the meantime, we all need some rest. It's been a long day."

Dinkum favored each of them with a long study. "You both need the hospital."

"I'm fine. It's Hailey I'm worried about." Chap let his gaze travel over her, frowning at what he saw.

"I'm okay. Really."

"You've got the makings of a first-class black eye, but it's your ribs I'm more worried about. I can tell they're aching. Did Klaverly kick you?"

She ducked her head. "Maybe. But I'm all right."

He slid a finger beneath her chin, causing her to meet his gaze. "Tell me that while you're looking me in the eyes."

She shook her head.

"I didn't think so. You're too honest to lie."

"I'll go to the hospital if you do. Your arm's got to be hurting where Klaverly cut it."

She had him there.

"Thank you," she said to Dinkum.

He looked surprised. "For what?"

"For worrying about me and Chap. It's been a long time—maybe never—since anyone's worried about me."

He averted his gaze. "Same as I'd do for anyone."

"Don't let him fool you," Chap said. "He's got a soft heart. Especially when it comes to you."

"I'll head back to the ranch," Dinkum said. "Unless you want me to stick around."

"No. Go on back. See that everything's all right and explain to the men that they're on their own for meals for the next while. We'll be along as soon as we get checked out at the hospital." Chap grasped his friend's hand. "Thanks, Dink. For everything. I don't know what I'd have done without you."

His friend looked embarrassed. "Hey, it was Sam."

Chap knew that, for Dinkum, that said it all.

Now, if only he could get Hailey to stop blaming herself and place the blame where it belonged, squarely on Lawson's head.

There'd be a reckoning.

At the emergency room, both Chap and Hailey were examined, including having X-rays taken of her ribs. "You've got two badly bruised ribs," a young doctor told her. "We can tape them up or you can let them heal on their own."

When she chose the latter, he added, "Most people heal just fine. Take it easy, no strenuous exercise for a few days. In the meantime, we'll see what we can do about those cuts on your face." He was tactful enough not to ask how she'd gotten them, though she sensed his curiosity.

He applied antiseptic to her cheekbone and jaw, gave her two aspirin and told her to take two more when she got home, and pronounced her good-to-go.

Chap had needed stitches for his arm and a tetanus shot.

"You two been in some kind of fight?" a nurse asked, concern evident on his face.

"Someone did his best to beat up the lady," Chap said, "and we've seen the sheriff."

"That right, miss?" the nurse asked.

"Yes." She didn't have the energy to explain. Apparently satisfied, the nurse nodded.

Chap wrapped an arm around Hailey. "Let's get you home."

She clamped a hand over a yawn. "I won't argue with you." Though only eight hours had passed since Klaverly had abducted her, it felt like sixteen. Every bone in her body ached, and even recognizing it as a cliché, she felt the truth of it.

The drive back to the ranch was noneventful. Hailey relaxed enough to close her eyes, but they popped open when she felt the truck swerve sharply. She saw they had reached a hard curve in the road.

She felt Chap tap the brakes, but nothing happened. Another tap. Harder this time. Still nothing.

He applied the parking brake to no avail.

"Chap—" Her voice quivered in the dark cab.

The narrow road, flanked by a canyon wall

on one side and a cliff on the other, left no margin for error. She took in Chap's dilemma. Turning too far in one direction would ram them against the unforgiving granite face of the canyon. Too far in the other would take them over the edge and down an equally unforgiving mountainside.

Patches of black ice had already made navigating the road dicey. Without brakes, it was deadly.

"Hold on," he said.

He didn't have to tell her twice.

The truck was careering down the road with no brakes.

"Up ahead." Hailey pointed to a cutout where truckers could steer their runaway trucks. Could Chap keep the pickup on the road until they reached it?

While he wrestled with the steering wheel, she did the only thing she could. She prayed.

The pickup came to an abrupt stop when its momentum died at the spot Hailey had pointed out.

A pent-up breath shuddered from her.

Long moments passed.

"Are you okay?" he asked.

"Fine." She was holding on by a thread so frayed that she feared it would snap any moment, but she was unhurt by the runaway truck ride.

Chap pulled out his phone. "I'm calling highway patrol, then Dinkum."

By the time they'd been checked out by EMTs and waited for a tow truck to arrive, Hailey was dead on her feet.

Another cliché, she thought absently. She appeared not to have a thought in her head that wasn't a cliché.

The events of the day had finally caught up with her. She'd been kidnapped, beaten up, and nearly frozen in a ramshackle cabin, not to mention surviving a runaway pickup barreling down the road.

One question pounded through her mind with unrelenting persistence.

"How did someone know we were even in town?" she asked. "It's not like we were advertising it."

"Except people at the sheriff's office, the vet's place, and the hospital," Chap pointed out.

"They'd have no reason to tell anyone." She paused, considered. "You think someone at one of those places could have alerted Lawson?"

"I think it's possible. Tomorrow I'll check with the sheriff, see if Klaverly got his call. Maybe that will give us an idea on what to do next."

Dinkum had showed up around the time the tow truck did. "I can't leave you two alone for a minute without you getting into trouble."

Hailey welcomed his teasing, even though she knew it was forced. Worry had darkened his eyes to coal-black; the lines fanning them had grown deeper.

"Thank you," she said quietly. "You rescued us again."

"Don't you know by now that I care about you?"

The simple words started the tears. She'd held them at bay until now, but she couldn't hold them back any longer.

Dinkum looked like he'd been poleaxed. "Boss," he said, pulling Chap away from talking with the tow truck driver. "Help."

Despite the tears, despite everything, Hailey felt a smile poke itself forward. "It's okay," she said.

Chap rushed to her side. "What's going on?"

"We were just talking and, all of a sudden, the waterworks started."

Dinkum divided a helpless look between her and Chap.

Hailey waved away the men's concern. "I'm fine. Dinkum just said something that brought on the tears."

"I didn't," the foreman said, looking horrified at the idea. "I promise I didn't."

"You were being sweet. That's all."

"Dink, quit being sweet," Chap ordered him, but she could see the fondness in his eyes when he looked at his friend.

"I promise." The fervency in his voice caused her to smile fully, but exhaustion now claimed her and she swayed.

Chap swept her up into his arms despite her protests. "We're getting you home."

The last word started a fresh wave of tears. He carried her to the truck.

Wedged between the two men in Dinkum's truck, she did her best to stay awake, but exhaustion had taken its toll and Hailey found herself struggling to keep her eyes open.

"It's okay," Chap said when she yawned for the third time. "You've earned yourself a rest. And it just so happens that my shoulder is available."

Before she gave in to the weariness that had her in its clutches, though, she had to say something. "Have you thought about why we came through everything today? Klaverly could have sold me to Lawson, but you stopped him. Sam could have died, but he didn't. Then there's the whole thing of the truck speeding down the hill. We could have been killed, but we weren't."

"I'll bite. Why did we survive?"

"Because the Lord was watching over us." She didn't press the matter, content with having planted the seed.

Hailey lay her head against his shoulder, but sleep didn't come immediately. It was impossible not to think how right it felt to lean against this man who had risked his life for her.

The direction of her thoughts caused her to abruptly sit up.

Leaning *against* a man was dangerously close to leaning *on* one. And she couldn't afford to do that. She was in Chap's life only temporarily. Pretty soon, they'd both move on and return to the life they'd had before she'd broken into his pickup. A small smile touched her lips as she thought of all that had taken place since then.

If she let herself fall in love with Chap, she knew what the outcome would be. Heartache.

NINE

Chap had felt Hailey fighting exhaustion and sensed when she finally gave in to it. He wrapped his arm around her more securely and felt her nestle into his side. He glanced at her profile, soft in repose.

Her features were finely drawn, yet there was strength there, too. Strength and courage. And unselfishness. She'd refused to go to the hospital to be checked out by a doctor until after they had checked on Sam.

When they arrived at the ranch, he helped Hailey inside and left her in the capable hands of Mrs. Heppel.

He retreated to the kitchen and made himself a sandwich.

Hailey's question about who knew they'd be on the road at that time rolled around in his head. Who had known he and Hailey were in town last night? The sheriff and a deputy.

Klaverly himself. The veterinarian and her assistant. The doctor and staff at the emergency room. Eight people. Nine if you counted a man waiting in the vet's office.

Not a huge number, but enough that it would take time to check on each of them. He'd known the veterinarian since he'd moved to the area. Vic Crane, the sheriff, was a newer arrival, but they'd always worked well together. As for the staff at the hospital, he had no reason to suspect them.

That brought up another question. Who had had the opportunity to sabotage the brakes? It wasn't a difficult task, but it did require some knowledge about cars.

Chap struggled to focus his thoughts, but he couldn't get past the terror of the last hours. Things could have turned out so differently.

Could Hailey be right about the Lord watching over them? The idea touched a forgotten place within him.

He didn't want to believe. Not anymore. But it gave him pause.

It gave him a great deal of pause.

What if the storm hadn't derailed Klaverly's plan on selling Hailey to Lawson, forcing them to take refuge in the cabin? What if Chap hadn't remembered the outlying cabin? What if Klaverly had succeeding in besting Chap in the fight? The what-ifs screamed through his head with unrelentingly persistence.

The last question tormented him with such heart-pounding force that he wondered the sound didn't wake everyone on the ranch.

With a brief knock, Dinkum let himself into the kitchen where Chap sat at the counter, nursing a cup of coffee. Though Chap had offered to have him live in the main house, Dinkum preferred bunking with the men. "Are you thinking what I am?" he asked.

Chap directed a grim look at his old friend. "That we nearly lost Hailey today."

"Got it in one. What're we going to do? That skunk Klaverly won't be the only one coming after her."

"No." And that scared him more than any runaway truck ever could.

"You can't protect her forever."

Chap wanted to argue with that. As much as he wanted to protect her for as long as was needed, he knew Dinkum was right. "We need to get her testimony in front of the grand jury, but I don't know who to trust. Plus, I don't think she's strong enough to face that. Not yet."

"She's stronger than you give her credit for," Dinkum said. "She was kidnapped and beat up, and all the while worrying herself sick about Sam, but she refused to give up."

Chap didn't respond. He didn't want to give voice to his admiration of Hailey. He had already lectured himself about the danger of having feelings for her. He'd do well to remember that.

At the same time, he couldn't shake the knowledge that he'd almost lost her today. That thought was going to keep him awake tonight. And in the nights to come.

In the kitchen the following morning, Hailey poured a cup of coffee, turned and offered it to Chap. He hadn't had to speak for her to know he was there. She doubted he ever had to announce his presence.

"What are you doing?" he asked.

Hailey looked up from where she was stirring pancake batter. "My job. I have twelve hungry men who want breakfast."

"You should have slept in. The men would have understood."

"You sure about that?" In truth, she needed to be up and working. Staying in bed had sounded appealing until reality set in and she started reliving the events of yesterday.

Work was an antidote to worry and fear.

She poured the batter onto a griddle. Feeding twelve men meant cooking on a large scale and doing it as quickly and efficiently as possible. There was no time to flip individual pancakes, so she had hit upon a system of making one gigantic pancake on a huge griddle, then dividing it into squares. The men didn't care that the pancakes weren't the traditional round ones; they only cared that there was plenty of butter and syrup to pass around.

"You're pretty amazing," he said.

Color invaded her cheeks; she felt it creeping up from her neck. "I'm just doing my job. Are we going to town to check on Sam today? Maybe bring him home."

"Yeah." Chap's expression clouded. "We need to make a statement at the sheriff's office, too."

"I know." Her shoulders slumped a bit before she straightened them. "When I finish here, I'll clean up and be ready to go."

"Okay."

Hailey knew that he wanted to spare her this. She also knew that it had to be done. Might as well get it over with.

After serving breakfast and cleaning up, she got ready.

They climbed into one of the extra trucks he kept at the ranch. Thankfully, the ride to town went without incident. When they reached the sheriff's office, she got a better look at it in the daylight. She supposed the design was efficient if not particularly appealing.

The thought of having to recount the events of yesterday sent her knees shaking, but she stiffened her resolve as well as her knees and prepared to do what was necessary.

The jail was almost too bright, the fluorescent lights casting weird shadows and turning everyone's skin a sickly green.

Chap reintroduced her to the sheriff, who immediately instructed Hailey to call her Vic.

"Victoria's too prissy," she said.

Hailey liked the woman who was a mix of brashness and femininity. She made her statement, grateful that she was able to tell her story without breaking down.

"And you had no idea that your fiancé was a murderer?" the sheriff asked.

"Ex-fiancé," Hailey stressed. "And, no, I didn't have a clue of who he really was."

"Tell me once more how Klaverly fits in," the sheriff said.

Hailey had already gone through this, but she appreciated the sheriff's thoroughness.

"He suspected someone powerful was after her, so he searched around town until the right people got wind of it and offered him money to bring her in. And he didn't waste any time, either." Chap's voice was tinged with impatience.

Vic sent him a reproving glance. "If you don't mind, I'd like to hear it from the lady."

Once more, Hailey recounted the story of Klaverly stabbing Sam, kidnapping her and holding her in the cabin. She couldn't repress a shudder. "When I think what would have happened if he'd managed to turn me over..." Another shudder.

"I understand," Vic said and turned to Chap. "News about this is going to get out fast. You know how the grapevine around here is. Gossip is what the town feeds on, especially come winter. I give it a day before this is all over town." She heaved a sigh.

"Probably less when Klaverly starts yammering about a lawyer," Chap put in.

The sheriff frowned. "I hate to be the one to tell you, but unfortunately, he escaped from jail. I've got two deputies who are going to be mighty sorry about that. It makes our department look bad, and I won't stand for that kind of incompetence."

Hailey felt Chap's displeasure, but he didn't say anything, only nodded and stood.

Fear shivered through her at the knowledge that the man who had abducted her had escaped, but she, like Chap, didn't say anything. She stood as well. "Thank you, Sheriff."

"No need. That's what I'm here for." The

sheriff shifted her attention to Chap. "I can't say how sorry I am about that skunk getting away, especially on my watch. We're short-staffed, and what with the usual tourist nonsense in the winter, I'm feeling a mite overwhelmed about now."

"Not your fault, Vic." But the tightness of his mouth and the clipped way he spoke suggested he felt otherwise.

Hailey started to leave but, on an impulse, turned back to offer her thanks once more. The sheriff had made the process easier than Hailey had anticipated, but what she saw in the other woman's eyes stopped her. A cold look had settled in the previously friendly gaze.

It was gone as quickly as it had appeared, and Hailey wondered if she'd imagined it.

Sam gave a joyful woof when he saw Chap and Hailey. They had gone to the animal clinic directly after leaving the sheriff's office.

"How're you doing, boy?" Chap asked, petting the shepherd's large head.

Another woof.

"I think he's saying he wants to go home," the vet said with a smile. "But we'd like to keep him for at least one more day. Just to be on the safe side. We don't want to take any risks with a traumatic injury like he's suffered.

Plus, there's always the danger of infection setting in."

While Chap understood her caution, he wanted to bring Sam back home today. He looked to Hailey on the other side of the table where Sam was lying. He knew she wanted him home just as much as he did.

"It has to be your decision," she said, "but I think the doctor is right. Sam's been through a lot."

He knew she was right. "Okay." Reluctance had him drawing out the word. "Anything he needs," he told the vet. "Anything at all."

She smiled again. "I know. He'll get the best care we can give him."

With a final pat to Sam's head, Chap left, Hailey at his side.

"I know that was hard," she said once they were outside.

"Yeah. I wish we could have brought him home today. He looked like he was wondering why we were leaving without him."

"I'm so sorry he was hurt defending me."

Chap heard the tears in her voice and reached for her hand. "You didn't do anything wrong."

"You're both heroes," Hailey said softly.

He held up his hand to ward off the words of praise. "I told you. I'm no hero, but Sam is."

"Okay," she said with a teasing smile. "I'll

keep that in mind for the next time you do something incredibly brave when the bad guys come after us."

He knew she meant the words to be light-hearted, but neither of them was smiling by the time she'd finished. The fact was there would be a next time. And a time after that, until she testified against Lawson.

Suddenly, Hailey grabbed his arm. "There." She took shelter behind a large truck. "That's one of Doug's men," she said, pointing to a tall, thin man loitering outside a hardware store.

"Are you sure?"

"I'm sure. How did he know we were in town?"

"We don't know that he does," Chap said. "Could be that he's just asking questions. Stay here. I want to get a little closer."

Chap crossed the street and pretended an interest in a bin of ice scrapers two storefronts down. When the man walked into the hardware store, Chap saw him talking with someone familiar. He slipped out and hurried back to where Hailey was waiting for him.

"What is it?" Hailey asked.

"I saw him talking with the sheriff."

What was Vic Crane doing talking with a man on Lawson's payroll?

In fairness to the sheriff, the meeting could

be totally unrelated to Hailey. Maybe a happenstance encounter of two people. But why was Vic there in the first place?

She wasn't on her rounds, not in the daytime. It was quiet during daylight hours, the cowhands who frequented the bars at work. Nighttime was another story. Crane preferred to patrol herself. Still, there could be any number of reasons for her to make a stop at the store. The two of them bumping into each other might only be a coincidence.

Except that Chap didn't believe in coincidences.

Believing in coincidences was a good way to get yourself and your buddies killed. Coincidences didn't hold up when you started to look closely. More often than not, they fell apart.

It had held true when he'd been deployed in the Sandbox, the soldiers' nickname for the Middle East, and had continued to hold when he'd joined the marshals and then S&J.

So why, Chap asked himself again, was the sheriff there in the middle of the day meeting with a man who was after him and Hailey?

TEN

Tension filled the cab of the truck on the trip back to the ranch.

Chap pointed to the tiny scar at the right side of her mouth." How did you come by that?"

Hailey knew he was trying to distract her from the knowledge that one of Lawson's men had been talking with the sheriff, but she went along with it. "It happened soon after I aged out of foster care and was on my own. I got on the wrong side of a broken bottle. It was late, and this boy, probably no older than me, wanted the park bench I had already staked out." She gave a lopsided smile. "I won, but I came away with this."

"You have an interesting past."

"Not really. I was in foster care, then on the streets before I found work."

"You didn't have any close relatives?"

She shook her head.

"Tell me about your job in Denver," Hailey said, wanting to deflect the attention away from herself and get to know Chap better. "S&J Security/Protection—is that right?"

"It's just what the name says. Shelley Rabb Judd and her brother, Jake Rabb, started the business years ago. They know that sometimes people need more help than what the police can give them. That's where we come in."

"'We'?"

"The operatives. Shelley and Jake recruit mainly from ex-military and law enforcement. Some of us knew each other in our former lives. We trust each other to have our backs."

"You like the work. I can hear it in your voice."

"Yeah, I guess you could say that. There's—" he appeared to search for the right word "—satisfaction in it. Knowing you're keeping someone who's been stalked or otherwise victimized safe. Making a difference. That and the ranch keep me pretty busy."

"What did you do before that?"

"I started off as a SEAL. When I left the Teams, I worked for the US Marshals for a few years, then as a special investigator for the federal prosecutor's office in Denver. I left after six months."

"Why did you leave so soon?"

"I got tired of working for people who were

more interested in getting convictions than in having them."

It was but one more sign of Chap's integrity, that he couldn't continue working for people more concerned with securing guilty verdicts than in doing what was right.

She tucked that away to be taken out and examined later.

"Not all prosecutors are that way," he said. "One of S&J's operators is married to a woman who made me start believing that some DAs really are interested in justice."

"She sounds special."

"She is that. Rafe got himself a winner." There was affection in his voice, that of a brother for a sister.

"Rafe?"

"Rafe and Shannon Zuniga. They bought a farm outside Denver. I'll introduce you to them sometime."

He sounded like there would be a *sometime* for them. A dart of pleasure zinged through her before she realized that it had most likely been a throwaway comment. Once her troubles were over, she and Chap would go their separate ways.

The pleasure of moments ago faded as Hailey accepted that reality.

What had she expected? Chap had promised

to keep her safe. That was all she needed from him. All she wanted.

That self-directed lecture given, she should have felt better. And wondered why she didn't.

When a loud popping sounded, Chap steered the truck to the side of the road.

A man less experienced with the report of gunshots might have thought that it was a tire blowout, but he knew better.

"Stay down," he said. "I'm going to check it out."

She did as he said and stayed low.

He returned in less than a minute, his mouth drawn. "Someone shot out the tire."

Her face blanched and he knew she understood the danger they found themselves in, but she didn't whine.

Instead, she said, "I can help change it."

He wanted to hug her for that, but he had to stay focused on the attack he feared was coming.

"And put ourselves square in someone's sights as we're wrestling with a tire? No. We're going to have to hoof it back to the ranch." He lifted his eyes to the sky, saw the darkening clouds.

"How far is it?"

"No more than five miles. Remember to stay

low. Whoever is out there is planning on picking us off as soon as we make a move."

As soon as they opened the doors, a shot pinged the front fender, reinforcing his warning.

"We can do this," he said. "At least you're not in an evening dress and sandals this time." His attempt at humor fell flat.

Once again, they were running for their lives. They reached a copse of trees. Fortunately, much of the snow and ice had melted, but the ground was still slippery.

Hailey slid and landed hard on her butt, letting out a yelp of pain.

Chap helped her up. "You all right to keep going?"

"Don't worry about me." But her next steps were tentative.

"You're a trooper."

"More like I know we can't stay here."

As though to confirm her words, a bullet tore up the ground at their feet. It had been close. Too close.

What he first took as a blessing—that the snow had melted a good deal—now proved to be the opposite. A thin film of ice had formed over the snow, making every step treacherous, and though they wore boots, they weren't enough to keep them from sliding.

The tree coverage was spotty, causing them to run from tree to tree, all the while dodging bullets. When they finally reached a small copse, she slumped against a trunk and drew in a long breath.

They needed to rest. He could keep going, but he could hear Hailey's labored breathing. So they'd take a minute and get their breath.

Chap reviewed their situation and didn't like what he came up with.

They were out of cell range, and even if by some wonder they were to get a bar or two, the thick canopy of snow-laden branches would no doubt block any contact.

The sour note of his thoughts must have showed on his face for Hailey said, "I know we're in trouble, but you'll find a way out. You always do."

He wanted to tell her that her faith in him was misplaced, but he couldn't shatter the trust in her eyes.

"We'll be fine." The lie stuck to his lips, and he hoped the words didn't sound as false to her as they did to him. Lying, even for a good cause like reassuring Hailey, didn't sit well with him.

She didn't respond.

"Thank you," he said, "for your faith. Faith is something I'm in short supply of these days."

"The men after us—they're the ones from that first night, aren't they?" she asked.

He nodded. "I'd say they're Lawson's first string. Someone must have called in some serious favors to get them released."

"He'll never quit coming after me." The despair in her voice had Chap wanting to tell her that Lawson would grow tired of the chase and forget about her. But he couldn't lie to her again. And Hailey wouldn't have believed him if he had. So he remained silent.

They were stuck with the truth. Unfortunately, the truth had a way of turning ugly sometimes.

"Thanks," she said.

"For what?"

"For not lying to me this time and for not telling me that Doug will give up."

He should have known that he hadn't fooled her earlier. The lady was too smart to be taken in, even by a well-meaning lie. "Sorry about that."

"It's okay. I know you were just trying to keep my spirits up."

The direction of the wind had changed and the snow now swirled in front of them. With the deepening sky as background, the effect was almost hypnotic. In the SEALs, Chap had worked as part of a team, each member doing his part to bring about a successful mission. S&J operatives normally worked on their own, unless the job was unusually big and required more operatives.

Chap had known some incredibly brave men and women during his time in the SEALs and in the marshals and then again at S&J, but never had he known anyone with as much pure grit as Hailey.

She had no training in survival, but she never let up. She simply did what needed to be done, asking as few questions as possible.

He wished he could tell her that they were out of trouble, that they'd lost the men chasing them, but the truth was, they were only postponing the inevitable.

As for Hailey and himself, they were losing ground. Though she did her best to keep up, she was reaching the end of her stamina. No matter how brave she was, she lacked the conditioning to keep going, particularly in the brutal cold.

If he were on his own, he would circle around behind the men and take them out one at a time. But he couldn't do that with Hailey here. While he was busy taking out one man, another could make his way toward her and take her, plus he didn't know how many men there were. Two? Three? More?

It was too risky.

Finding a place to stash her, as he'd done in the woods on the night he'd met her, was the answer, but there was no way he would leave her on her own. If only he had Sam with him.

Chap shook his head to clear it of chilling scenarios. If those men got their hands on Hailey, she would be taken to Lawson and then killed. But not before the man had made her suffer first.

They needed to find shelter, but there was none to be found. And then he remembered; a cabin, built by a city family for weekends of roughing it was somewhere close by. Not liking what "roughing it" had entailed, they had abandoned the place years ago. To his knowledge, it was still standing.

Could he find it in the storm? Landmarks were obscured, markings long since covered by ice and snow. He'd last seen the cabin from a distance several years ago and now had only a vague idea of where it was located.

They didn't have a choice. He'd grabbed Hailey's hand and started in what he thought was the direction of the cabin when gunfire punctuated the late afternoon. They hunkered down and stayed that way until the shots died off.

"Don't worry," he said. "We're headed to an

old cabin that's been abandoned. We can get warm there."

What he hadn't told her was that what came next made this look like a cakewalk. They had to cross a stream to get to the cabin. That meant walking on a sheet of ice and hoping it was frozen solid.

It couldn't be helped. He'd never been one to shirk what had to be done, only gritted his teeth and done it.

Hailey tried to keep up her spirits, but when another round of gunfire had them scrambling for the ground again, she admitted that she was losing the battle. What's more, she'd sprained her ankle in their mad dash for cover. It wasn't broken, but it was painful enough to slow her down. The last thing she wanted was to be a liability.

"We'll be all right," Chap whispered.

She heard the worry in his voice.

"I'm trying to believe that, but we're pinned down. They have men and weapons on their side, and my ankle—" She stopped. She hadn't been going to tell him that she'd injured her ankle. He had enough worries.

"You hurt it. Let me see."

Given the temperature, she couldn't remove

her boot. Regardless, he took her ankle in his hands and felt it through the leather.

"It's hard to say, but I'm guessing it's a sprain."

It might as well have been broken, she thought, for all the good it would do if they had to run.

Another barrage of shots peppered the air.

"Keep down," Chap ordered.

"No worries."

"I'm going to draw their fire. When I do, I want you to make it to the trees."

"What about you?" It didn't take much figuring to understand that he was going to make himself a target to give her the opportunity to escape.

"Your ankle will slow you down. You'll need the diversion to make it." His voice turned gruff. "Don't worry about me. I can take care of myself."

"So can I. I'm not leaving you."

"Don't you get it?" Gruffness was now replaced with harshness. "You're a liability. I'm better off by myself."

Pain lanced through her before she realized that he was being deliberately cruel to convince her to leave. "Not going to work," she said. "It seems like a hotshot ex-navy SEAL could figure a way out of this. Or don't your skills work on dry land?"

She set her jaw and prepared to wait him out. They were in this together.

"We're going to crawl our way out of here," Chap said.

Crawl? Whatever she'd expected, it wasn't that. The ground was freezing. They risked hypothermia if they remained there for any length of time.

"We're going to crawl our way to safety?" she asked, unable to keep the disbelief from her voice.

"The fog is thicker on the ground. If we're quiet, they won't see us. Probably."

"Probably?"

"Yeah. Probably."

"Okay."

"Then let's go."

Like that, they were on all fours, scuttling their way over the colder-than-cold ground.

The slow pace was made even more so by the lumps and bumps of ice-encrusted snow they encountered. Fresh snow would have been more easily navigated. As it was, the hard ground pulled at their clothing, ripping it and letting in the frigid air.

At last, they got to their feet. It was a relief not to be crawling on the ice-cold ground any longer.

When Hailey lagged, he paused.

"Sorry," she said, "had to catch my breath."

"No problem."

But there was. The fog was breaking up bit by bit. Soon, the men chasing them would be able to see them.

Hailey thought she'd known what real cold was. The night she and Chap had stumbled through the woods during a blizzard with Doug's men chasing them, she'd been as cold as she'd ever been. But this set a new record.

Her breath came in short, hard gasps. Winded from the exertion and the cold exacerbating it, she didn't know how long she could keep moving.

She had to keep going. If not for herself, then for Chap. She knew he wouldn't leave her. His code of honor wouldn't permit it. She also knew that she could get him killed if she didn't step up her pace.

So she picked up one foot, planted it in front of the other, and then repeated the process. If she didn't allow herself to think, maybe she could keep moving. She didn't give herself time to register her numb fingers or feet that felt like blocks of ice.

"You're doing great," Chap said.

That was a lie, and they both knew it. She nodded, unable to respond. Not when she needed every bit of energy she could muster to lift her feet in the stumbling shuffle she'd worked out to move in a forward direction.

Chap had to be as cold as she was, but he wasn't letting it slow him down. His spirit was one of dogged determination. She brought every bit of determination she had to bear to a single goal. Do. Not. Give. Up.

As she did her best to keep up with Chap, she had a kind of déjà vu moment of running through the woods with him on that first night. Would she ever be able to free herself from Lawson's henchmen? Right now, it didn't appear likely.

He turned back to give her a quick nod of approval. It warmed her even as the harsh wind buffeted them from all sides. When a particularly strong burst knocked her over, she lay there, trying to catch her breath.

A strong hand reached down to pull her up.

"Someday maybe I'll be able to return the favor," she said.

"Don't worry about it. For right now, all we have to worry about is getting to that cabin."

She strained to hear him over the wind.

What were they going to do? In her mind, she went over the options. Wait it out and pray Lawson's goons got tired of tromping around in the cold and gave up the search. Show themselves and fight their way out.

The only problem was that they were outmanned and outgunned.

Hailey placed a hand over her stomach, a vain attempt to still the fluttery whisper of dread that had settled there. She couldn't afford to be sick. She and Chap had enough to deal with as it was.

The frost of their breaths mingled in the subfreezing air, creating a small plume of fog. She wanted to smile at the sight, but she was afraid she'd cry instead. Once she started, she wouldn't be able to stop.

As if reading her thoughts, Chap touched a finger to her lips. "It'll be okay."

"Will it?" Dreaded tears threatened to spill over.

"Sure."

The frigid temperature plus the incessant wind made a formidable enemy. That's what she needed: to think of the weather as the enemy. She could and would defeat it.

The shooting had halted, but they weren't out of trouble yet.

They pulled to a hard stop when they came to a stream.

"The water looks frozen," Chap said. "The trick is knowing if it's frozen solid. It looks like the ice will hold, but I can't know for certain. One way or another, we have to cross it. It's that or go back and face the men chasing us."

She inhaled deeply. "Let's do it."

"You sure?"

"We don't have a choice, do we?"

"No."

He hadn't soft-pedaled it. She supposed she should appreciate that. "You're afraid I'm going to buckle, aren't you?"

"No. I know you'll do what you have to," he said, and she clung to his faith in her. "Are you ready?"

No, she wanted to yell over the wind, but she only nodded.

Armed with prayer, she took her first step onto the ice.

ELEVEN

Chap didn't fool himself into thinking it would be easy to traverse the ice. Crossing any body of water, even a relatively small stream, in winter, and especially in these conditions, was beyond risky. Doing so without the proper equipment was a fool's move, but they didn't have a choice. It was either that or face the gunmen who were showing no signs of letting up.

Though he and Hailey had managed to elude the men for the moment, he knew they would find the trail soon enough and be back on the hunt. In the SEALs, he was accustomed to being the hunter. Being on the other end of the equation rubbed him the wrong way.

With her lighter weight, Hailey had a better chance of making it across the ice than he did.

"Slow and easy is the name of the game," he said. "We're back to crawling again." He sympathized with her grimace. "We'll be able to distribute our weight better if we're on all fours," he said.

"Do I just wait for the ice to crack all the way and for me to fall in?"

Hailey's tart words lifted his spirits. If she could joke at a time like this, they'd make it.

So far, so good. He glanced at Hailey, gave her a thumbs-up.

And then it happened.

A splinter of sound. Not overly loud, but enough that he knew instantly what it was.

When he felt the ice shift beneath him, he knew it was cracking. He was going under; that was a given. If Hailey stayed where she was, she'd go under as well.

"Move," he told Hailey. "Get away from me."

She moved several feet away, but then she stopped. "What are you going to do?"

He didn't answer. The crack had already expanded. In the time that one heartbeat segued into the next, he fell into the frigid depths of the stream, which was really a river beneath the layer of ice.

Immediately, the cold leached into his every pore. If he hadn't known it wasn't possible, he'd have said that the frigid water wasn't really water at all but an ice floe that sucked him in and refused to let go.

It cut through him like shards of glass, each slice excruciating in the extreme. He'd survived winter warfare training in Alaska, but this took cold to new heights. His heavy clothes worked against him, dragging him further down.

Don't lose the hole.

The words chanted through his mind, their rhythm the only thing that penetrated the glacial cold permeating every fiber of his being.

If he lost the hole—the portal to above— he was doomed. There was no way he could punch through the ice to forge a second opening. The combination of frigid water and sheer exhaustion tempted him to let go and drift into the darkness. It would be easy—so easy—to let go.

No.

Giving up wasn't in a SEAL's wheelhouse. Feeling as though he was fighting his way through a sea of freezing honey, he succeeded in pushing an arm upward and caught hold of the edge.

Barely.

Even his thick gloves couldn't prevent the jagged ice from biting into his fingers. The cold had numbed his mind as well as the rest of him. If only he had a tool of some kind that he could use as a claw to dig into the ice and anchor him.

Could he make it the rest of the way? His purchase on the ledge was slipping, and he feared he didn't have enough strength to lift himself up and over. Darkness chased after him; he was ready to give in to it.

But he'd reckoned without Hailey. Hunkered down on her knees, she caught his wrist just as he was about to go under. Somehow, he'd managed to keep his head above water, but he knew he wouldn't be able to hold on much longer.

"I've got you," she yelled over the raging wind.

"You can't hold me."

"Don't tell me what I can and can't do." She got to her stomach and wrapped a second hand around his arm.

He held on as though his life depended upon it—which it did.

Her grasp was slipping, his weight too much for her. If she kept at it, she'd be pulled under, too.

"Let go. You can't pull me out. We'll both die."

"No way, cowboy. We're both getting out of here. Now shut up and help me."

Hailey didn't give up. No matter how much her arms and shoulders must hurt, she just kept pulling. Again, he wanted to tell her to let go, but one look at the set of her chin convinced him to keep the words to himself.

With Hailey's help and, using every ounce of what little strength he had, they managed to lift him far enough that he could prop his elbows on the ledge of ice. He finished pulling himself up the remainder of the way.

They both lay there, panting, struggling just to breathe. The battle against the ice had cost them, depleting their energy. Just as concerning, he was now soaking wet. He needed to raise his body temperature, and that wouldn't happen in his drenched clothes.

Hypothermia was bound to set in unless they found somewhere warm and he could put some heat into him. But first they had to get off the ice.

"Turn over," he said, "and spread-eagle."

Progress was measured in inches rather than feet as they crawled their way across the ice. Even so, they were making headway, though the other side still looked impossibly far away.

He was reminded of the story of the tortoise and the hare. Slow and steady won the race. They were winning. Or they would be, if the cold wasn't seeping into them with every second they spent on the ice. With so much of the body flush to the surface, they were soaking in the cold at an alarming rate.

His wet clothes only intensified the freezing temperature, and though Hailey hadn't gone in the water, she had gotten plenty wet in pulling him out.

"We can do it," she called to him.

"I know." His voice was fading, a sign that he was losing strength.

When they reached the other side, they helped each other up the bank. Together, they staggered a few feet away and collapsed.

"We have to get up," she said.

"Ha…half to get up," he repeated. Had he said the words aloud? He wasn't sure. He couldn't hear anything over the roaring in his head.

He pushed to his feet. Or he thought he did. But, no, he was still lying on the ground, a murky mix of snow and dirt. How had that happened? He tried to remember but couldn't put the events together.

"Chap. Chap, can you hear me?"

Of course he could hear her. Why was she yelling at him? Lethargy was beginning to set in. That, his indistinct speech, and inability to hold on to two consecutive thoughts, told him he was already in the grips of hypothermia.

Hailey appeared to be faring slightly better

than he was, but that meant little. Her speech, too, was growing slurred.

He tried to get to his feet. Failed. He tried again and this time made it. Barely.

They stumbled forward, but his awkwardness in putting one foot in front of the next caused him to trip. When he took a hard fall to the unforgiving ground, the impact shook him to the core. He feared he didn't have the strength to get up.

He was certain it was over for him, but Hailey tugged at his arm and helped him to his feet.

She gave his elbow a comforting squeeze. At least, he thought she had. His thinking was sluggish. If he could have summoned the energy to laugh, he'd have done so at the understatement. His thinking was far past sluggish. It had stopped altogether.

"We have to keep going," she shouted over the wind. "If we stop…"

He didn't hear the rest of the words, but he guessed it was something to the effect that if they stopped, they'd never be able to start again.

The cabin had to be close. Or had he underestimated the distance? In the snow, it was easy to miscalculate.

"There." He pointed to what looked like a cabin.

Only, it wasn't. It was just a tree. His eyes were playing tricks on him. Or maybe it was his mind. He didn't know.

And that scared him more than anything.

Hailey darted worried glances Chap's way. She knew he was rapidly falling prey to hypothermia. So was she.

She was beyond cold. Numbness was beginning to set in, not just in her movements but in her thinking. Her mind felt muzzy; it was difficult to hold onto a thought before it danced away. Her steps dragged until she wasn't certain she was walking at all.

She did her best to blank her mind to the frigid cold that turned her feet into leaden blocks. Her legs were no better. They didn't want to work. She told them what to do, but they refused.

They pushed their way forward, each step an exercise in grit. Only the idea that they'd eventually reach shelter gave her the strength to keep going.

She squinted through the snow and made out a rough-looking structure. "There," she said and pointed.

Chap didn't respond.

With a strength she didn't know she possessed, she slipped a shoulder beneath his arm and half carried, half pushed him the remaining few steps.

She shouldered open the door, relieved to find it hadn't been locked. Inside, she slammed it shut, grateful that the latch caught. The cabin was small, smaller than her bedroom at Chap's house, but, to her, it looked like a palace. The furnishings included a rough-hewn table, two chairs and a sofa that looked like it might have been from the Truman era.

The howl of the wind penetrated the walls, but at least they were no longer in its claws. The relief was enormous. Even better, there was a fireplace, already stacked with wood.

The first order of business was to warm them up. She helped Chap take off the jacket, which was soaked clear through, and settled him in a chair. She then got to work starting a fire, giving thanks to her time on the streets when she'd lit fires in trash cans for warmth. When heat filled the room, she thought she might cry.

She knew Chap wanted to sleep but also knew that was the worst thing for him. Not yet. Not until he warmed up. After rummaging inside a cupboard, she came away with a beat-up pot and a couple of mugs. Though she hated to brave the outside again, she took the pot and filled it with snow. It was torture to return to the bitter cold, but she didn't have a choice.

Inside once more, she let the heat from the fire soak into her.

She draped her coat over the back of a chair and did the same with Chap's.

Using her scarf to hold the pot handle, she held it over the fire until the snow melted and the water began to boil. There was nothing appealing about hot water except that it was hot.

She poured it into the mugs and handed one to Chap.

His hands trembled so badly that he could barely hold it. She guided the cup to his lips. "Not too fast," she cautioned.

He took a sip then another.

Satisfied that he could drink on his own, she took a small drink from her own mug and felt the warmth spread through her.

They finished the water, and she set about seeing if she could find any clothes for them. She tested a door at the back of the room and discovered it led to a small bedroom. She stepped inside, found a narrow bed and, wonder of wonders, a chest of drawers filled with men's clothes.

"Chap," she called. "Come see what I found."

When there was no answer, she went back

to the main room and found him slumped in the chair.

She slid an arm under his shoulder and helped him up. When they reached the bedroom, she sat him on the bed and began undoing his shoes, then pulled off his socks.

He pushed her away. "I can take off my own shoes and socks." At least that's what she thought he'd said. His voice was so slurred that the words sounded like those of a toddler just learning to talk.

He didn't need gentleness right now. He needed to get warm. So she put a measure of tart in her voice. "Glad to hear it. Can you get out of those wet clothes on your own?"

He nodded and made a shooing gesture to her.

She grabbed some clothes for herself, then left the room, shutting the door behind her.

Five minutes later, dressed in jeans and a shirt that swallowed her whole, she tapped on the bedroom door. When she didn't get an answer, she opened it and found Chap dressed in the borrowed clothes and lying on the bed. The bed would certainly be more comfortable than the lumpy sofa in the living room, but he needed warmth more than comfort, and that meant being close to the fire.

She returned to the front room and, with a

great deal of grunting, dragged the oversized sofa so that it was near the fire. In the bedroom, she helped him up and into the living area. There, they walked back and forth in the small space.

"Tired," Chap mumbled.

So was she, but she kept at it for a few more minutes until she was satisfied that they had warmed their muscles. She didn't want him to become overexerted and settled him on the sofa. She retrieved the bed's one blanket, returned, and lay it over him.

"Hailey..." With that, he closed his eyes.

Chap had risked his life for her over and over. It was time she took care of him.

Chap dreamed.

Men chasing Hailey and himself. Gunfire. And then the bone-deep cold.

Now it was the cold chasing him. Relentless. Unforgiving.

When he woke, he shook off the remnants of the dream and decided he felt almost human. Almost.

It was still dark, but he knew he wouldn't be going back to sleep. Too many things swirled through his mind. Evading their pursuers. Falling through the ice. Hailey saving him.

He looked down at the unfamiliar clothes.

Where had he gotten them? Then he remembered. Hailey had found them, had insisted he put them on. She'd done everything in her power to bring him back from succumbing to the hypothermia that had nearly done him in.

He saw her on a hard-backed chair, asleep. Her face was smudged with dirt. Shadows deep enough to get lost in framed her eyes. She looked fragile. But there was a tensile strength to her that said she would not be broken.

He noticed that she didn't have a blanket, had given the only one to him. He got to his feet and carried her to the sofa. There, he placed the blanket over her.

The fire had died, so he brought in more wood and started it up again. After seeing to the fire, he reviewed what was likely to happen. The men who were after them weren't going to give up. They had probably holed up somewhere for the night, but they'd be back on the hunt. It wouldn't take much time for them to see the smoke from the cabin and know where he and Hailey were.

That meant they had to be ready.

Their pursuers probably wouldn't attack until just before dawn. That was the optimum time to stage an attack, whatever the circumstances.

Hailey stirred, rubbed her eyes and sat up. "Chap? Are you okay?"

"I'm good. Thanks to you. You saved my life." His gaze was full of warmth as it rested on her. "You should have left me when I told you to."

"Would you have left me behind?"

"That's different."

"What's so different? Because you're a man and I'm a woman? Sorry. That one won't fly. And isn't there something in the SEALs about leaving no man behind?"

She had him there.

"Woman, you're as stubborn as a three-legged mule."

"A three-legged mule. Where did you get that?"

"If there's anything more stubborn than a four-legged mule, it's a three-legged one." The levity vanished from his voice. "You don't quit, do you? It would have been easy back there to just give up, but you kept going."

"The Lord hasn't quit on me. That's what keeps me going."

He wanted to automatically reject that but paused, considered. "If it helps you to believe that, go for it."

"But you don't believe."

He shook his head. More with regret than

with anger. "I quit on the Lord when He quit on me."

"I'm sorry."

"Don't be. I'm doing fine on my own."

Sadness filled her eyes, though she didn't argue with him. "You know about my past 'love,'" Hailey said. "Do you have someone special in your past?"

Did he want to share that part of his life with her, to relive the greatest failure of his life? He had done his best to push Lori from his mind, but the memory was there, he feared, to stay.

Chap shook his head, more to help him see more clearly than in answer. "There was someone," he said, voice so hoarse that it sounded like a croak.

Pictures of Lori flashed through his mind. Lori dabbing paint on his nose when they were redoing her apartment. Lori laughing as they built a snowman together and she pushed snow down his jacket. Lori making a face when she tried his first attempt at cooking risotto.

He tried to blink away the memories as he would a grain of sand irritating his eye, but the memories wouldn't be blinked away. They were there to stay. In truth, he didn't want to erase them. They were the best part of him; a part he wanted to cherish and hold close to his heart.

But before he knew it, he was telling Hailey of Lori, how she'd died at the hands of a man out for vengeance. "My fault," he concluded. "If she hadn't been with me, she'd still be alive. I was the target. Not her."

"You're too smart to believe it's your fault. She died because someone wanted you dead and got her instead. That's on them, not on you."

Chap had told himself the same thing, but he'd never been able to convince himself of the truthfulness of it. "I want to believe that, but I can't get the picture of her bleeding out from my mind. I knew Winston was gunning for me, but I thought I could handle it. I was too arrogant to think anyone could take me out." He laughed hollowly. "Turns out, I was right. He didn't get me. He got Lori. If I'd really loved her, I'd have stayed away from her. As far away as I could."

"Do you think Lori blamed you?"

"No." He knew that she wouldn't. Lori had had a forgiving heart as tender as his was now hard. But her family had blamed him. He'd done his best to comfort her mother and sister, but his words had been hollow, especially since he'd needed comfort, too.

"What about the Lord? Do you think He blames you?"

"The Lord and I aren't on what you'd call speaking terms these days." He wanted to turn away from Hailey, away from the compassion he read in her eyes, but he forced himself to keep his gaze level with hers.

"You might ask God about that before you write Him off. He forgave those who crucified Him. Why wouldn't He forgive you?"

Why wouldn't He?

Chap didn't know. He had consciously turned away from God and from the teachings of his childhood. How could he believe in a God who had allowed an innocent woman to be murdered?

He'd witnessed countless atrocities when he'd been deployed, had beheld acts of cruelty so vile that he'd been brought to his knees in tears, and had emerged resolved to do his best to prevent more.

But Lori's murder had shaken him to his core.

"How can you keep believing after all that you've been through?" he asked. "Losing your parents when you were hardly more than a baby? Moving from foster home to foster home? And now your ex-fiancé's trying to kill you."

"How can I not? The Lord has preserved me, despite everything. How can I deny His hand in my life?" She shook her head. "I know He's watching over me. Look at how He put you in my path at the exact time I needed you."

Chap wanted to tell her that it was only by happenstance, but the certainty in her words nearly caused him to reconsider his disbelief.

"You're pretty amazing."

She didn't try to deflect the compliment and only smiled. "The Lord is the amazing one. I'm just one of His children." She paused. "Like you." She placed her palms on either side of his face.

Tender feelings slow-walked their way through every part of him at her touch, and he wanted to hold her hands where they were, to hold on to their warmth against his cheeks.

But he couldn't.

He needed to keep a sensible distance between them. If he didn't, he wouldn't be able to think rationally. More important, he might very well give in to the feelings Hailey stirred within him.

When Lori had been murdered, he'd promised himself that he wouldn't get involved with another woman. The risk of losing someone he cared about, of the unspeakable pain if something happened to her, was too much.

No one had made him feel what he was feeling now since Lori.

Gently, he removed Hailey's hands from his face and took a step backward. "Thank you." He resisted the urge to squirm.

Navy SEALs, ex or not, do *not* squirm.

He shoved the conversation and feelings it stirred in him away. Right now, they had other problems. Problems like how they were going to get the better of the two men pursuing them.

It would soon be dawn. "The men chasing us haven't given up. I've got two handguns, and they've got automatic rifles. We're going to have to make them come to us."

"How do we do that?"

He explained his plan, while at the same time using his knife to cut a gash in his arm and letting it bleed onto his shirt to set the stage. He finished just as shots rang out, shattering the window, and he pushed her to the floor.

"How's your acting?"

TWELVE

Breathe in.
Breathe out.
Repeat.

Hailey focused on taking in one breath and pushing out another. It was the only thing she could control, so she concentrated on that. Her adrenaline spiked and she did her best to hide her rapidly unraveling nerves from Chap. He was depending on her. The last thing she wanted was for him to know how truly terrified she was.

When he had outlined his plan, she'd been certain he was joking.

"Remember," he'd said, "when the men show up, you have to sell them on the idea that I'm badly injured and close to dying. Don't be afraid to let them see that you're scared."

"No problem there," she muttered under her breath.

"Have I told you that you're one outstanding woman?" he asked.

"No."

"Remind me to do it once we're out of this." The stomping of heavy feet told her that the shooters were almost upon them. "Showtime."

She edged open the door and shouted, "Please. Don't shoot. My friend's been hit. I think he's dying."

Hailey pitched her voice to be heard outside. It wasn't easy, given the howl of the wind and the fact that her throat had turned scratchy, but she did her best. "Please. I'll come with you voluntarily if you'll only help him."

"Lady, you better not be trying to fool us." One man's voice carried back to her.

"I'm not. I promise."

She infused every bit of fear she could summon into her voice. It wasn't really acting, as she was truly terrified.

Had they bought her act?

"Throw out your gun," a voice called.

Chap motioned her to take the Beretta holstered at his ankle.

She tossed the gun out the door.

"Get away from the door."

A man pushed the door open and walked into the cabin, weapon drawn. The other kept his gun trained on her from a slight distance.

"You have his gun," she said, her words close to a sob. "Please help him. I don't want him to die." She pointed to the red stain on Chap's shirt. "See? He'll bleed out if we don't help him."

He looked at her in disbelief. "Lady, you don't get it. We don't want to help him. We want you. If he's dead, so much the better." He motioned for his partner to join him.

"He can't hurt you. He's unconscious. You might as well help him. Please." She steeped the word with every bit of pleading she could summon, even though it hurt to beg these men for anything.

Hailey had no illusions that they intended to help a wounded Chap. On the contrary, she knew that they were only trying to decide whether to let nature take its course or to finish him off now.

Either way, she understood that she would be the prize.

Chap was up for the biggest acting job of his life. Playing dead.

The gun at the small of his back was his backup. That, plus Hailey. She'd played her part like a pro. Now it was his turn.

Hailey continued to put on a convincing act. "You can see that he's near dying. Please help him. Then I'll go with you."

"Lady, like I told you, we're not here to help

him, but I'll do both you and him a favor and put him out of his misery."

"You'd shoot a helpless man?"

"Without blinking," he said. "For the trouble you two caused us, I'd shoot you right now, but the boss said to bring you back alive."

Out of the corner of his eye, Chap saw Hailey edge back a step. She grabbed the pot and slammed it over one man's head.

Chap sprang to action and twisted the other man's wrist until he dropped his weapon. He picked up the gun and aimed it at him.

"Get his gun," he told her.

She took it from the man she'd hit and gave it to Chap. He stood, keeping both guns trained on the two men.

They were dressed for long distance hiking in heavy coats, hats and snowshoes. They each carried a pair of poles, which were helpful in navigating through the snow.

"Take off your jackets and snowshoes," Chap ordered. The man Hailey had smacked with the pot was just coming around and looked stunned, as though he couldn't understand the reversal of positions.

With much grumbling, the men did as Chap said.

Chap gave one of the guns to Hailey. "If either one of them moves, shoot him."

"Gladly."

He went through the packs the men carried. Inside were thermoses, candy bars and packages of trail mix.

Near the bottom of the packs, Chap found what he'd hoped to find. Lengths of rope. He motioned the men to the chair and, after having them fold their arms behind them, bound their hands behind their backs and their ankles to the chair legs. He set aside one coil of rope to take with him and Hailey, then replaced it in one of the backpacks.

After testing what was in the thermoses, he took a swallow of hot chocolate. The rich sweetness soothed the pain of an empty belly. He handed a thermos and package of trail mix to Hailey. "Eat up. We're going to need the energy. We still have a ways to go."

"You don't need to tell me twice."

They both tore open the packages of trail mix. The combination of nuts, dried fruit and chocolate was just what they needed to restore their energy. They then wolfed down a candy bar apiece. Pleasure exploded on his taste buds.

"Glad you fellas came prepared," he said after putting down two candy bars.

"Hey," one man objected. "Those are ours."

"Shut up, Max," said the other.

"Tell them your name, too, why don't you?"

the one named Max said, sarcasm heavy in his voice.

"You'd leave us here to freeze to death?" the first man asked.

Chap threw him an unconcerned look. "In a heartbeat. I wouldn't worry about it if I was you. Someone will find you. Sooner or later."

He gestured to Hailey to put on one of the jackets and the snowshoes.

She put the jacket on over her own, then strapped on the snowshoes. When she fumbled with a strap, he stooped to help her.

"Thanks."

With the snowshoes enabling them to walk over the snow rather than tramp through it plus the poles they'd taken from the men, the trip should have been easy.

Of course, it was anything but.

Hailey took a cautious step forward. Another. Walking in snowshoes wasn't easy, but it beat trudging through the snow in shoes or even boots. The trick was to develop a rhythm. After a few tries, she had a system down and was able to keep up with Chap.

Mostly.

The poles helped her to keep her balance. When the terrain changed, the ground pockmarked with depressions, she nearly fell. When the inevitable happened and she tripped, landing on her back, she lay there a moment, trying to catch her breath.

"Turn on your stomach," Chap said. "Then pull a knee up in front of you."

She did as he instructed.

"Now, pull the other knee up."

With a few more maneuvers, she managed to get herself up.

"You look like you were born to snowshoe," he said.

"Hardly. But it sure covers the miles faster than walking."

They kept up a steady pace, and her confidence grew. Until her foot went through the snow, along with the rest of her. It was the same foot with the twisted ankle from last night's chase. One second she was on top of the snow, and the next she was underground. Was she in some kind of mine?

There was precious little light from above, and she blinked in the darkness.

"Hailey. Hailey."

She fixed her attention on Chap's voice.

"Are you all right?"

Experimentally, she tried her limbs and found that they all worked. "I think so."

"Hold on. I'm throwing down a rope."

She recalled that there had been ropes in the

men's backpacks and that Chap had saved one to put in his own.

"Wrap it around your middle," he called down, "then knot it as tight as you can. Brace your feet on the side of the wall."

She realized she couldn't do that with her snowshoes on and awkwardly removed them in the small space. She managed to stick them in her backpack and prepared for the ascent.

"Ready," she called up.

While Chap pulled, she "climbed" up the wall.

At the top, she fell to the ground. "Thank you."

He helped her up and then took the rope off her. "It weren't nothing, ma'am," he said in a thick drawl that teased a faint smile from her.

"You saved my life. Again."

"I'd say we saved each other." Though his words were light, his voice was not. There was something deeper in it. She would take it out and examine it later, but they still had ground to cover now.

She'd managed to pick up another layer of dirt while in the mine shaft. She was longing for a shower, anything to wash away the grime of the last day. She must look a sight.

"You're beautiful," Chap said, apparently guessing at her thoughts.

She'd held out against tears while she and Chap were being chased through the woods, as they were crossing the ice, and when she was in the mine tunnel, but she couldn't stem them now. "You say that now? When I'm covered in muck and mud? My hair is so filthy that it will probably never come clean. And you choose *now* to tell me that I'm beautiful?" Her voice rose with every word.

Despite the cold, she took off her gloves to swipe at the tears making rivulets down her cheeks.

"You're beautiful." When he repeated the words, the tears came harder.

How could he say that? Her hair was matted to her head. Her clothes were muddy.

"It's all right," he said and cradled her to him.

No, it wasn't, and she feared it would never be all right again. At last, she found the strength to pull away. "I'm sorry for that. I can't seem to stop crying. I'm not usually that weak."

"Don't sell yourself short. You're not weak. Far from it. You're stronger than you think."

"Thank you. I needed to hear that." Afraid she'd never be this courageous again, she lifted her hands to cup his face. "You're a good man. The best I've ever known."

He looked stunned, as though her words had caught him unaware, and she chastised herself for giving voice to those feelings.

But he didn't say anything, only took her hand. "We'll get through this. That's a promise."

Hailey mulled over Chap's words as he helped her on with her snowshoes once more. Was she stronger than she thought? There had been a time when she'd believed herself strong, capable, but that was before Doug had undermined her self-confidence, before he had convinced her that she didn't have any class or style. Bit by bit, he had taken over her life, making decisions for her, right down to how she wore her hair and what clothes she chose.

Chap was the opposite, building her up, but, at the same time, allowing her to stand on her own. Her feelings for him were growing by the day. With fresh resolve, she reminded herself of the recklessness of giving in to them.

Chap didn't talk much on the remainder of the trek home. Something about the way Hailey's hand had fit in his had sent off an alarm in his brain. He needed to think through what had just happened. Not only about evading the men intent on killing him and taking Hailey hostage but about what had happened between them. If he hadn't come to his senses in time, he might have done something unbelievably foolish. Like kiss her.

An hour later, they stumbled into the ranch house.

Sam greeted them. Chap hunkered down to wrap his arms around the shepherd. "It's good to have you home, boy."

Hailey did the same.

Sam licked their faces as though he couldn't get enough of them. If he had died, Chap knew a part of him would have died as well.

Dinkum was there, a phone at his ear. He hung up and glowered at them. Beneath the intimidating frown, though, lay genuine concern. "When I wasn't worrying over the two of you, I brought Sam home. Figured you'd be glad to see him."

Chap stood and clasped his friend's hand. "Thanks, man."

Mrs. Heppel fussed over them, took their outer clothes away to be washed, and returned to bustle Hailey upstairs, leaving Chap alone to explain to Dinkum what had happened.

"You two attract trouble like a politician attracts lies," Dinkum said. "I sent the men out in pairs to find you, even called the sheriff when you hadn't returned by midnight."

The sheriff. That was another thing to ponder. Chap still hadn't come up with a good reason for Crane to be talking with one of Lawson's thugs.

"The sheriff said she'd sent out some search parties. Seems as if you and Hailey managed to get home on your own."

Chap filled in his friend on what had happened since yesterday morning.

Accepting that they were up against too much now to take on themselves, he decided to call the state police to report the two men tied up in the cabin. After giving the officer a quick rundown of what had taken place, he almost asked about Vic Crane but decided against it. What could he report, anyway?

An hour later, Chap and Dinkum set out for the truck. Before seeing to the tire, he searched the area for shells. Spent casings littered the ground.

Making certain he didn't touch them with his bare hands, Chap slipped on crime scene gloves, which he routinely carried, picked them up, and sealed them in a plastic evidence bag he'd brought along for that purpose.

"Do you think you'll get any prints?" Dinkum asked.

"I doubt it, but you can never tell. Maybe someone got careless."

His friend only nodded. "How did you get across that river?"

"A lot of prayer."

Dinkum shot him a curious look, but Chap didn't elaborate.

He thought back to Dinkum's remark about calling the sheriff. What would have happened if one of Crane's search parties had found them, Chap wondered. Would he and Hailey have been rescued or would they be lying in a ditch somewhere?

THIRTEEN

Hailey scrubbed herself until her skin was raw. She wished it was as easy to wash away the knowledge that the man she'd once believed she'd loved hated her so much that he'd sent killers after her.

Doug would get what was coming to him. As soon as she gave her statement to the proper authorities, he would be arrested. If she lived long enough to make the statement, that is.

She pushed that away. Negative thoughts wouldn't help.

What Chap had told her about Lori had touched her unbearably. She understood enough to know that he didn't share those memories easily. Somehow, knowing that he'd trusted her enough to share them with her had forged a bond between them.

She could nearly feel the weight of the tremendous sorrow radiating through him, like heavy chains, crushing the life from him.

That was love.

Whatever she'd felt for Doug hadn't been love. Infatuation. Pleasure in no longer being alone. But love? No. Not even close.

Why had she ever thought those shallow feelings she'd entertained for him could be love?

Lack of experience, yes. Lack of example of the real thing, most certainly. Even more, though, was her total aloneness. She'd been so desperate for someone to love and to be loved by that she'd grabbed the first opportunity she'd encountered. It was a counterfeit, though. Never again would she accept something so false.

"I'm sorry for your loss," she had told him. The words were woefully inadequate. Why couldn't she think of anything more meaningful to say?

"It's over."

But it wasn't, she thought, recalling the lines of grief that had etched themselves in his face. Grief like that didn't vanish. Grief and love were two sides of the same coin.

What would it be to know love like that? To know that a man loved her with his entire being?

She shook her head at the question. She wasn't likely to know. In the meantime, she had a job to do.

When she showed up in the bunkhouse kitchen, the men greeted her with cheers.

"We sure missed you, Hailey," one said. "You don't know what it was like around here without you."

"You mean without my cooking, don't you?" she teased.

"I mean you. You make everything better." His expression turned serious. "We were out looking for you and the boss most of the night. If something had happened to you—"

"I'm fine." Immeasurably touched, she blinked back tears. "Thank you. Now, let me get to work." She made a shooing motion. "I promise something special for dinner."

"Yes, ma'am!"

With a lighter heart, she set to work. She'd have enough time to make stuffed pork chops and twice-baked potatoes, if she hurried. She would then round out the meal with salad, rolls and a quick dessert.

Humming a tune that even she could hear was woefully off-key, she split the pork chops, made the stuffing, and put them together.

When Chap and Sam joined her, she was able to smile fully, something she hadn't been able to do for more than a day.

"You look better," he said.

"I couldn't look much worse."

"Dinkum and I changed the tire on the truck and brought it back to the ranch."

Her smile slipped a bit as she replayed the events of yesterday in her mind. "That's good."

"Hey," he said, "we made it. That's what matters."

"I know. I guess I'm still a little shaky after everything."

"There, on the ice, you saved my life. I wouldn't have made it without you."

She tried for light. "Just returning the favor for all the times you've saved my life."

"You could have died pulling me out of the river." His voice had sobered.

"But I didn't. Like you said, we made it."

"We make a pretty good team." Consternation crossed his face.

She had no response and left it at that. "Yeah. I need to get dinner fixed, so…"

"Got it." Chap took himself off, obviously as ready to abandon the conversation as she was.

We make a pretty good team.

The words stuck in her mind as she prepared the rest of the meal.

Fool.

What had he been thinking, telling Hailey that they made a pretty good team? Obviously, he hadn't been thinking.

Maybe he could be excused for letting his feelings get the better of him. She'd looked so adorable in an apron that cinched her narrow waist and with a smudge of something on her face.

What must she have thought? He could only hope that she hadn't paid the words any attention. The intriguing thing about getting to know a fascinating woman was the journey to discover what made her so...well, intriguing. Not that he was interested in her in a romantic sense. Of course not. But it didn't hurt to make a new friend.

And that's what Hailey was. A friend. Nothing more. The part of him that longed for love had died along with Lori. It was better that way. If he didn't allow himself to feel the sweet heady joy of loving another woman, he would never again endure that kind of pain if that love was taken from him.

With that settled, Chap told himself he felt better. There'd be no more trips down a path that only brought heartache.

But he had bigger things to worry over now. Things like whether he should contact the state police with his suspicions about Vic Crane. All he had was witnessing her talking with one of Lawson's men.

By no stretch of the imagination could that

be conceived a crime or even suspicious. An accidental meeting. The man could have been asking her about places to rent. Only, no one wanted to rent a place in the high country during winter unless it was for skiing and there were no ski resorts in the area.

Questions bounced around in his head until he couldn't concentrate. In the end, he decided to call and ask a couple of casual questions. He had a good relationship with one officer, Jake, in particular. Before getting to the subject, he asked if the conversation could be kept on the down-low for the time being.

"If that's what you want," his buddy said cautiously.

Chap tried to phrase his question in a casual manner. "What can you tell me about Sheriff Vic Crane?"

"What makes you ask?"

Chap sensed something there. "No real reason. Just wanted to get your take on her."

"There's been some talk about her," the officer said after a long hesitation, "but nothing definitive."

"Okay… Thanks."

"If you hear anything, you'll let us know." This was no longer a conversation between friends but one between a law officer and a civilian.

"You can count on it."

Next thing on his agenda was getting help from S&J. Except for his calls to Josh Harvath, he'd resisted asking until now, but he couldn't do this alone. The danger was escalating, and, though he'd accepted there couldn't be anything permanent with Hailey, he had vowed to keep her safe.

He called the lab division of the company and told the woman in charge that he'd be sending in bullets from a crime scene for prints. Then he contacted Shannon Zuniga of the DA's office. He spent a few minutes asking about her family's vacation.

"Okay, Chap. I appreciate you asking about our trip, but I know you didn't call to ask about the joys of traveling with two toddlers. What's up?"

She listened as he related Hailey's story and what had happened since she'd witnessed Lawson murder a man.

"My best advice is to get her to a US attorney," Shannon said. "They'll take it from there.

"And don't forget you have a standing invitation to visit. We'd love to see you." She and Rafe owned a ranch where they raised llamas, goats, chickens and children.

"Thanks, Shannon. I appreciate it. I'd like to see you, too."

He knew his friends were worried about him, as were other friends at S&J, but he hadn't had the energy to hide his grief over Lori's murder, but he was going to lose other people he cared about, too, if he didn't stop alienating himself. He pressed his fingers to his temples and allowed himself to revel, for a moment only, in the memory of her. Her smile. Her touch. Her voice.

Then he put away those precious images in the invisible box he kept locked inside of him.

Hailey heard a commotion at the kitchen door. She knew Mrs. Heppel had gone shopping. It was only her and Dinkum at the house. Had he gone out for a moment?

When she saw the foreman walk into the kitchen, she relaxed, but only for a moment. He was closely followed by Bob Klaverly.

"Hailey, get out of here," Dinkum said. Blood ran down his face from a nasty-looking wound on his forehead.

"Not if she wants to see you stay alive," Klaverly said.

The foreman made an abrupt move and turned to punch the man in the jaw. Klaverly didn't lose a beat. He fired at Dinkum, the bullet hitting him in the gut.

"No!" Hailey ran to Dinkum, terrified by

the blood blossoming on his shirt, but the former ranch hand yanked her by the hair and pushed her aside. "You try to help him and I'll shoot him again."

"Please. Let me stop the bleeding." Hadn't they done this dance before when he had stabbed Sam? Now this poor excuse for a human being was exacting the same pain from her, holding someone she cared deeply about to bend her to his will. She gave a silent thanks that Sam had gone with Chap and was out of harm's way.

The look on Klaverly's face was one of undiluted hatred. "You thought you was rid of me, didn't you?"

He looked and smelled like he'd been living in the woods. A heavy growth of beard darkened his face. His breath smelled like a bear had crawled up and died inside his mouth.

She couldn't let Dinkum bleed to death. She had to get help, and that meant taking on the man who had already proved the lengths he was willing to go to bring her to Lawson.

Hailey flung herself at Klaverly and succeeded in taking them both to the floor. She pummeled him with her fists. When he drew back his arm and slammed his fist into the side of her head, she nearly lost consciousness.

It was fury, not fear, that had her scrabbling

backward. When she got to her feet, her hand closed over the handle of the pot of soup simmering on the stove. She heaved it at him, scalding him in the face.

He screamed—a banshee sound as primitive as he looked. "You burned me!"

Klaverly had threatened her, bullied her, and kidnapped her. No way would she let him take her without a fight.

He swiped at his face then aimed the gun at Dinkum.

Hailey stepped between them. "You want to take me to Lawson alive? You won't get a chance if you shoot me, and that's what it's going to take if you try to hurt him again. I'll fight you with everything I have until you won't have a choice but to kill me." She met his glare without flinching. "You let me see to him and then I'll go with you."

"No, Hailey." Dinkum's barely-there voice scraped at her heart.

Klaverly ignored the foreman and spit at her. "If that's the way you want to play it."

"That's the way I want to play it." She got a dish towel and pressed it against Dinkum's wound. Then she tore the tie from her apron to hold the towel in place. There wasn't anything more she could do.

Klaverly yanked the cord from the toaster

and, taking no risks with her, roughly tied her wrists together. Uncaring that she didn't have a coat, he shoved her outside and pushed her to an unfamiliar-looking truck. "Get in."

"How am I going to do that with my hands tied?"

He lifted her into the truck and strapped the seat belt around her. She knew it wasn't concern for her safety on his part that prompted the gesture but to further restrain her.

The roads were clear, and he drove quickly, obviously knowing where he was going. When they crossed the state border, he turned west. Any hope that he wasn't taking her to Lawson then died.

"How do you know where to take me?"

"I got a call giving me directions."

A call? That was interesting. Who would have known enough to call him? The only people who knew Klaverly had kidnapped her were the sheriff and a couple of deputies.

And then it made sense.

An hour later, they arrived at Lawson's house. After parking, Klaverly dragged her to the front door. Once checked out by a guard, he pushed her inside. "Here she is. Just like I promised." He gave her another small shove forward.

Lawson—she could no longer think of him

as Doug—greeted them and raked his gaze over her. "A man who gets the job done. I like that." His voice grated on her. How had she ever thought it strong? It sounded oily, slick. Like the man himself.

He closed the short distance between them and reached for her arm, pulling her to him.

Even bound and bloody from the fight with Klaverly, she refused to cower before him and stared up at him defiantly.

Lawson had taken so much from her. She wouldn't let him take this small scrap of dignity from her, too.

Klaverly focused his attention on Lawson. "I brought her to you. Now I want the money I was promised."

"Do you think he…" she paused to sneer at Lawson "…is going to keep his word?"

"Sure he will. He's got no cause not to."

"You're more stupid than you look if you believe that."

"Watch your mouth," the man she'd once believed she'd loved said. "Or maybe you prefer I just stick a gun in it." The contempt in his eyes caused a cold shiver down her back. "You always were smart. Under all that naïveté, there was a good brain. There was a time I thought maybe you'd throw in with me. Together, we'd be unstoppable. But then I saw you were too much a Goody Two-shoes to ever use those smarts of yours the way I wanted."

He gestured to the goons standing like two sentinels at the doorway. "You know what to do with him."

Fear lit Klaverly's eyes. "No. I was promised a pile of money if I brought the woman to you."

"Are you really that stupid?" Hailey's ex-fiancé pulled a gun. "Do you want me to kill you here? Or do you want to go with my boys? Buy yourself another few minutes?"

Even though Klaverly had beaten her and kidnapped her—twice—Hailey didn't want to see him murdered. Not like this.

"You're a pig," she said, addressing Lawson. This time he backhanded her, hard enough to send her to the floor.

Lawson only laughed. "You're as stupid as he is. You were never anything to me other than a good-looking woman on my arm." He jerked at thumb at Klaverly and then pointed to his men. "Get him out of my sight. He makes me sick." He held up a hand. "Never mind. I'll do it myself."

With that, he shot Klaverly in the heart.

FOURTEEN

Hailey was missing.

Chap had returned home to find her gone and Mrs. Heppel close to weeping. "It's Dinkum," she said. "I'd been out doing some shopping and when I returned it was to find him on the floor, bleeding. I called 9-1-1. An ambulance took him to the hospital. I was getting ready to go there myself."

He took in the overturned chair, the soup spilled on the floor, the saucepan tossed aside, the signs of a struggle. "Have you seen Hailey?"

She twisted her hands. "No, sir. I wish I'd never gone to the store."

Chap didn't have time to comfort her except to say, "It's not your fault."

"Do you want to go with me?"

"No. I'll need my truck. When you get there, stay there." Though he doubted whoever had shot Dinkum would return, he didn't want his housekeeper there alone.

Sam gave a plaintive woof, obviously wanting to go with him.

Chap patted the shepherd's head. "Not this time, boy. You're still recovering."

He made short work of getting to the hospital and demanded to know what had happened to Dinkum. He didn't realize how loud his voice had gotten and how much of a scene he was causing until two security guards appeared.

But before they could try to escort him out of the hospital, a doctor appeared. He waved the guards aside and turned to Chap. "Your friend's being operated on."

"Did he say anything before you put him out?" Chap asked.

"Only one word. 'Klaverly.'"

That confirmed his worst fears. Klaverly was going to sell Hailey to Lawson. He had to find her, but he had no idea where to start. Then he remembered Vic Crane's talk with one of Lawson's men.

He intended to pay a visit to the sheriff to see what she had to say.

Only, she wasn't in the office when he stopped by, and the deputy told him that she'd taken some personal time.

With fear for Hailey nipping at his mind, Chap headed back to the truck. When he pulled out onto the street, he saw Crane's personal vehicle drive by. From the glimpse he'd caught, she was in civvies rather than uniform.

With no other lead, he followed her, staying far enough behind to keep her from spotting him.

"Okay," he said to himself. "Let's see where you're going."

Crane drove first south and then east until she'd crossed the state line. Hailey had told him that Lawson's main residence was in Fort Collins, Colorado, a college town only sixty miles from the border.

When Crane pulled in at a gas station, Chap drove on by, then circled back and parked on the far side of the pumps. He could still see her, but she would have to strain to notice him. She went inside and returned a few minutes later, a large cup and small bag in her hand.

A snack to see her through until she reached her destination, he guessed.

He continued to shadow her until she turned up a private drive. Okay, he wouldn't be following her there. He found a place to park. The driveway turned out to be a road leading up a hillside. Avoiding the road itself, he hoofed it up the steep incline and came upon what appeared to be a compound. The main house extended with wings on either side. A barn, maybe an equipment shed, a huge garage and various other outbuildings sat in the background.

Now what?

He saw Crane had left her car in an honest-to-goodness parking lot off the main house and was now walking to the mansion.

Did it belong to Douglas Lawson or had he, Chap, just wasted several hours of his time?

He slipped behind a tree until she entered the house. And waited.

"Well, well, well." Vic Crane skimmed her gaze over Hailey. "Look who we have here."

"No thanks to you," Lawson said.

Crane ignored him. "You think you're so special, don't you?" she asked Hailey.

"Not special," Hailey answered, "just someone who has better taste in friends than others."

The sheriff drew back her arm and slapped her.

Hailey stumbled but kept to her feet. "Klaverly didn't escape on his own, did he? You let him go. That way you didn't have to get your hands dirty by coming after me yourself. And it was you who tampered with the brakes on Chap's truck."

"It didn't take much to convince Klaverly

to go after you. He was always jealous of Chap and pretty bitter about working for him. I made sure the men who set the fire found him. When he botched taking you, I released him. I couldn't have him talking. If he'd been any kind of a man, he'd have gotten the job done the first time.

"As for the brakes, I saw how the wind was blowing. Chap was never going to think of us as any more than friends. Why not take him out while I got rid of you?" She advanced on Hailey again, but Hailey was too fast and moved in. She struck out with her leg, hitting the sheriff in the chest and sending her sprawling.

Crane got to her feet, but before she could strike again, Lawson pulled her away. "Much as I like a good cat fight, we have some matters to address, matters that can't wait.

"You," he said to Crane, "you could have taken her any number of times, but you didn't."

"I was playing my role," the sheriff snapped back. "You wanted me to keep on the right side of things in that Podunk town. I couldn't very well have kidnapped her, not with Chapman watching her every minute."

"Or was it that you didn't want Chapman to see who—or what—you really are?" Lawson shrugged. "No matter. One of my moles at the state police said that Chapman was asking questions about you, which caused them to run a background check. You're no good to me now." With no fanfare, he pulled his gun and shot her in the heart, just as he had Klaverly.

Though Hailey shouldn't have been shocked, she couldn't contain a gasp. Lawson had killed Klaverly and the sheriff with as little thought as he had the man who had stolen from him.

Lawson sent her his patented smile; the one that used to make her melt with love for him. Now it only made her skin crawl.

"Don't worry over Crane," he said. "She's been dirty for years. I planted her and people like her in towns all over Wyoming and Colorado and New Mexico."

When Hailey lifted her chin and stared at him, it was with revulsion. "You're nothing but a cheap killer. All your swanky clothes and lavish parties won't change that. I wonder what your fancy friends would think of you if they could see you for what you are."

"Keep it up, honey, and I'll fix that pretty face of yours so that no one will ever want to look at you again."

She kept quiet after that. No sense in angering him. He liked to brag about himself, so she let him. His narcissism would have been comical in another situation. Now, she saw it as a way to buy some time and encouraged him to tell her how he had put together the second-to-largest crime syndicate in Colorado/Wyoming.

"I was doing it right under your nose. You didn't have a clue, did you?" he taunted.

"No," she said. "I didn't have a clue." For that, she blamed herself. She would never understand how she hadn't seen him for who he really was.

Chap would come for her. She didn't doubt it. But would he come in time? He didn't even know where she was.

"You're so obvious. Asking me questions, waiting for your cowboy to come and save you. But I won't fault you for buying yourself a little time. Besides, you make a good audience. All that little-girl innocence and so enraptured with me. I think that's why I chose you to begin with."

"You never cared for me at all, did you?" She didn't shrink from the scorn in his eyes.

"You were the perfect foil. Who'd suspect that a naïve little fool like you would choose someone mixed up with organized crime? People look at you and see guilelessness, and they think the same about me."

"You were using me all the time." Despite everything she'd learned about him, she still struggled to wrap her mind around it.

"Hey, you got what you wanted out of it. You went to the best restaurants, shopped at the best stores."

"I never cared about those things. You were the one who wanted them. I wanted a home and children." It was all Hailey could do to keep the tears from her voice as she thought of the family she would never have.

"I didn't lie. You'd have given me a son. He'd take over the family business when he was old enough."

Nothing he could say could have chilled her more. The idea of her child being raised by such a man turned her stomach.

"And if he hadn't wanted that?"

"Of course he would. He'd follow in his old man's footsteps."

"I'd kill you before I let that happen."

Whatever happened to her couldn't be as miserable as the life he had just described. She shuddered even thinking about being tied to a man like Doug Lawson, trotted out like a show pony whenever he needed to play the happily married man. There would be no children; she couldn't bring innocent children into such a marriage.

Lawson wagged a finger at her. "Don't turn your nose up at it. It would have been a good life for you. You'd never have to worry about money again. You could have shopped for beautiful clothes and worn the most expensive jewelry. All you would have had to do was smile for the cameras and then go back to your perfect world."

She stuck out her chin. "It sounds like a prison. A velvet-lined prison. I'd rather be scrounging for scraps on the streets than live in a cage, especially with you as my jailer."

He tut-tutted. "You missed your opportunity. Now you'll die because of it." He gave a menacing smile. "Do you know that it's hard to get away with murder? But making someone disappear? That's the ticket. A murder is always going to come back to get you.

"When an adult disappears, the police like to make it easy on themselves. They'll spend time looking for the person—at first. Then the case grows cold, the leads dry up, and the good officers of the law decide that the person went away on his or her own."

He tossed a careless glance her way. "I have plans for you. I want you out of my hair. For good." Lawson rubbed his knuckles along his jacket, the gesture so full of arrogance that it made her sick.

"You have to know that Chap will be looking for me."

"I'm counting on it. I'll get rid of both of you in one day."

The confidence in his voice gave her a chill. She didn't doubt that he'd do exactly as he'd said.

She didn't respond. He was so certain that he had her cowed. He couldn't know that she was only biding her time. And her rage.

He had lied to her. Probably even mocked her to his friends. But the hurt she'd experienced upon learning that he'd never loved her had evaporated. In its place was enormous relief that she hadn't tied herself to such a man.

She could really pick them, couldn't she? Something cold lurked within the same eyes she'd once thought so appealing with their long dark lashes. Now they gleamed with cruelty.

Hailey threw herself at him and slammed her knee into his groin, using every ounce of strength she could muster.

He spat out a crude word. It looked like he might crumple, but he shook himself and, with a roar, came at her, fists raised.

She attacked him, using every move she'd learned on the streets. She clawed and bit and yanked at the perfectly styled hair.

Lawson punched her in the jaw. As she fell, the cliché "dropping like a stone" came to mind. Blackness swirled around her, a misery of motion and murky colors. She wasn't certain if she'd passed out or not.

He then kicked her in the ribs. She must have held on to some consciousness because a vicious pain registered, and she curled up in a ball.

With her last bit of strength, Hailey pushed herself up to her knees. She detested being in this subservient position to a man she loathed with her whole being, but she couldn't make it any further.

"I like seeing you this way. On your knees, begging me for mercy." He laughed rudely. "It's a good look on you."

"I'm not begging. For mercy or for anything else. Not from you."

He pulled a gun from his waistband. "You should be. You're a nothing. That's why I chose you in the first place."

Rage coursed through her. If only she could turn the tables on him, he would be the one begging.

Lawson yanked her to her feet then punched her in the jaw. "This is the only thing you're good for."

Her whole face throbbed. She probably had a couple of loose teeth.

Lawson shoved her ahead of him.

She willed her feet to move, one in front of the other.

He prodded her with the barrel of the gun. "Look at you. Moving right along. I'd say that I'm proud of you, but why bother? You're a nothing, and you always will be. I'd almost consider keeping you around for a while, just so I can have the pleasure of reminding you of that."

Hailey half turned. "I can't believe I almost married you." she said more to herself than to him.

His face twisted into an ugly scowl. "You better watch it, *sweetheart*. I might just decide to give you the same thing I gave your friend."

The features she'd once found so attractive were repugnant now. The too-handsome face with its weak jaw, the eyes that could beam with sincerity filled with malice, the thin mouth that had once touched hers with what she took to be love twisted in a sneer. She'd seen what she'd wanted to see.

He preened. "I'm handsome, rich, powerful. You could do a lot worse."

His arrogance nearly caused her to claw at him with her bare hands. She longed to punch him in that face he was so proud of, a face now filled with a smarmy smile, but she couldn't, not if she wanted to play the part of a weak, spineless creature. She'd show him that she was anything but.

When he punched her hard enough to make her head snap back, she couldn't take it any longer and launched herself at Lawson. He slapped her hand away but not before she scratched his cheek with her nails. Four long gouges now marred his carefully cultivated winter tan.

He put a hand to his cheek and snarled when it came away bloody. "You're going to regret that."

"Do your worst."

He called his men into the room. "Tie her hands, then take her to the barn," he ordered. "You know what to do."

The one named George stared at her, eyes so full of cruelty that she wanted to run, even knowing she had no place to go. He bound her hands behind her with a rough piece of rope he'd pulled from his pocket.

They dragged her to the enormous barn on the south side of the property.

When they reached the barn, she turned and kicked George in the knee. He roared at the pain, then backhanded her. "You're asking for it, lady."

Inside the barn, his partner swept away a layer of straw, then pressed a small indentation in the floor. A small section gave way, revealing an underground box, not much bigger than a coffin.

Then she got it.

They were going to put her in there.

"No!"

She fought against George, but her efforts were next to useless with her hands tied. Finally, she reared her head back and hit him in the chin. Given the difference in their heights, she didn't have much leverage, but she gave it all she had.

His yowl gave her momentary satisfaction, but not much.

He cuffed her at the side of the head and she fell to her knees. He then kicked her in the ribs, pushing her into the box.

"See how you like it in there." He and his partner shared a mean laugh.

When the lid closed, she couldn't hold back the tears. Crying wouldn't help; it would only use up the little oxygen she had, and she did her best to stifle the tears.

Think.

Was there some way to push against the wooden lid that sealed her inside? With her hands shackled, she had little strength with which to lift it, but she tried. Tried and got nowhere. Even if she managed to dislodge the lid, there was still the barn floor to contend with.

It was hopeless.

Not even Chap could find her here.

A bolt of fear speared through her, more terrifying even than being buried in the box. Lawson wasn't one to leave loose ends, and he'd see Chap as a loose end.

If Chap was hurt or… She inhaled a sharp breath. Killed…it would be on her. The image tormented her until she couldn't bear it.

Seconds—or was it minutes?—later, she was startled into awareness. Had she blacked out? For how long? She had no way of telling time.

She banged against the wood as best she could with her bound hands, that she was wasting her oxygen. She forced herself to stop and lie still. If she was to survive, she needed to be smart.

But she couldn't help the little sob that escaped.

Chap watched as two men took Hailey to the barn. Within a few minutes, they left. Without Hailey.

When they returned to the house, he ran to the barn, opened the massive door and began to search for her. He paused. Did he hear a faint banging?

After identifying its location, he hunkered down and spread his hands, searching for a latch or a seam. At last he found it. A faint line in the floor.

A small notch allowed him to pry the floorboard open. Inside was a rough-made wooden box. He used his knife to break open the latch.

What he saw had his heart clenching. Hailey.

He lifted her out, then gently lay her on the floor. She was so still that he feared she wasn't breathing.

Suddenly, the prayers he'd thought locked away for good burst forth. "Please, Lord, don't let Hailey die."

When had he found his faith in prayer again? Was it when Hailey had prayed in the vet's office that Sam would recover? Or when she'd shared her belief in the Lord that morning in the cabin? Whenever it had happened, he gave thanks for it.

She made a soft sputter of sound.

"Hailey. Hailey. Open your eyes, honey."

Another sputter before she opened her eyes.

"It's going to be okay," he said, unclear as to whether he was reassuring her or himself.

"Did I hear you praying?" she asked as he cut the rope binding her hands.

"Maybe." He wasn't up to discussing his newly found faith right then.

There, on the dirty floor, he held her. Just held her. After a few minutes, he helped her to a standing position. It was then that he heard the unmistakable sound of a pistol being cocked behind.

Slowly, he turned, hands outstretched.

"This can go down in one of two ways," the larger of the two men said. "One, we kill you both here and now. Two, we take you to Lawson and let him kill you."

"Take off," Chap told Hailey. "I'll keep them busy."

She shot him a look that said she wasn't going anywhere, and while he appreciated her bravery, there wasn't much she could do. She was unarmed and had recently been unconscious.

"I'm not leaving you." She squared her shoulders. "I can hold my own."

He watched her stand slim and straight, uncowering in the face of a man twice her size. Fierce determination and undaunted courage radiated from her in nearly palpable waves of energy. Even with several feet separating them, he could feel her resolve.

The men attacked, exploding into action with a flurry of fists and feet designed to inflict maximum pain and to intimidate.

Okay. Maybe they weren't as professional

as Chap had first supposed. Real profession-
als wouldn't waste energy on showy moves
like that. They would simply get the job done.

He blocked a flying kick from the first man
then grabbed his ankle and twisted it so that
the man was left with only one leg to balance
on. Predictably, he toppled over.

But the man didn't stay down, springing up to
come at him from a different angle. Chap didn't
let the man get near enough to land a blow.
Standing over six feet five inches and probably coming in at a good two hundred and-fifty
pounds, a blow from him could take anyone
out, even a highly trained SEAL like himself.

Chap feinted a move to the left and then
pivoted so that the man's back was now facing him. With a hard jab to his lower back,
Chap connected and got in a crippling blow
to his kidneys.

His opponent spun around, but not without a
cry of pain. Enraged, he came at Chap again,
fists raised and fire in his eyes.

Chap noticed him favoring his side. The hit
to the kidneys had slowed him down. Chap
pretended to cower, forcing the guy to come
to him. When his opponent aimed a fist at
his face, Chap ducked then came back with
a short-arm punch, catching him in the jaw,
causing him to stagger.

Good.

He risked a glance at Hailey, saw that she was parrying thrusts from the second man. Resolution radiated from her. She was a warrior, ready to take on any and all challengers.

He had to get to her, but his man wasn't finished yet. What did it take to bring him down?

It was then that Chap noted the man tilting his head to the side. Could he have a glass jaw? *Find the enemy's weakness and then use it*. A weak jaw that could be easily broken would take the man out for sure.

The man's eyes narrowed as though he could read Chap's thoughts. The goon wouldn't be giving him the opportunity to get in another blow to his jaw.

Chap aimed lower and kicked the man at the side of the knee. The knee was a delicate joint. A blow in the right place could bring down even the biggest opponent.

He got in a good kick to the vulnerable side of the knee, and the man fell to the floor, but didn't stay down. Instead, he got to his feet and came at Chap with fresh fury, one that promised retribution.

FIFTEEN

Chap had told her to take off while he was keeping Lawson's men occupied, but Hailey had no intention of doing that. No way would she leave him on his own to face the two men who probably topped five hundred pounds together.

She sized up her opponent. She was no match for the man who looked at her like he'd like to have her for breakfast and then use her bones to pick his teeth, but she'd do her best to put up a good fight and keep him from joining his partner in attacking Chap. She had to stand and fight. She spread her feet, right foot slightly forward, and prepared for battle.

When he lunged at her, she danced out of his way. The taunting gaze with which he'd raked her told her that he was only playing with her. Well, he'd see that she could play, too.

But for how long? She had no illusions that

she could fend him off indefinitely. Though not as big as Chap's opponent, he was plenty big.

She only had to stop him from making her his breakfast until Chap could finish off his man and come to her aid.

"C'mon, little girl. Let's see what you've got."

"What I've got," she said with deliberate precision, "is a big load of contempt for men like you."

His eyes narrowed. "You've got a mouth on you. No wonder the boss wants you dead."

She ignored that. She needed to think, not trade quips with him. But he had a hundred pounds on her. How was she supposed to beat that?

He came at her, grabbed her arm and twisted it. Spasms of pain screamed through her arm and shoulder. When he loosened his grip, she managed to wriggle from his grasp and turned to face him.

She got in a solid blow to his solar plexus, and was gratified when he gave an oomph of pain. Following up with another punch to his midsection, she then struck out with her leg and caught him on the upper thigh, a particularly vulnerable section of the leg.

He howled, telling her that she'd hit her spot. *Good.*

Though inflicting pain wasn't something

she liked doing, she'd do whatever it took to stay alive. These men had no intention of letting her and Chap live.

She saw Chap delivering blow after blow to his opponent. The determination in his eyes gave her strength when her attacker moved in once more. He swung back his arm, his intent obvious.

She ducked and came in low.

He sidestepped, and she missed her opportunity to get in another blow to his leg. "You're gonna be sorry you got out of that box."

She didn't react. As it was, she had all she could do to avoid his punishing fists.

"Maybe this will do." She straightened and struck out with her elbow, catching him on his side. The angle was awkward, but she managed to connect.

Though he gave her a dirty look, the expression in his eyes also held reluctant respect. "You've got some moves on you. I'll give you that. But you're gonna regret hammering on me."

Before Hailey could react, he wrapped his arms around her midsection, lifted her off the ground and held her there, suspended. With her arms caught against her sides, she didn't have any leverage to free herself.

Her head was at a level with his shoulder,

and she raised it just enough to slam the top
of it into his chin.

With another yowl, he released her, dropping her to the ground.

She landed with a thud, the wind knocked
out of her, but she couldn't afford to congrat-
ulate herself.

Her opponent was now well and truly angry.
He came at her, rage in his eyes and jaw set
with such rigid determination that she took a
step back. Another. His intent was obvious.

He was far bigger than she was and had obviously had some training, but he'd learn that
she wasn't to be underestimated. When he got
within a few inches of her, she pushed the palm
of her hand up and out, jamming it into his
nose.

Without missing a beat, she was on him,
using her fists to pummel his face. And though
her hands weren't exceptionally big, they were
strong from years of mixing, stirring, and sliding huge pans into an oven.

Even so, he pushed her off as though he was
swatting away a fly, sending her to the ground.

She refused to give in. When the man moved
closer to her, she braced herself on her elbows
and struck out with her right leg, thrusting her
foot into his gut with all her might.

His oomph of surprise gave her a fleeting

satisfaction as she quickly got to her feet. His snarl banished any self-congratulations, and she knew all she'd done was infuriate him. She snuck her left leg behind his right knee, causing him to falter and giving her a moment to think.

Hailey studied him, noticed that while he was fast on the attack, he wasn't as quick on the carry-through. She could use that to her advantage.

This time when he lunged at her, she didn't dance away. Instead, she held her ground until he was almost on her. Then she sidestepped, letting his momentum carry him down. The hard-packed ground made for an unforgiving surface. When he didn't immediately get up, she hoped he'd been momentarily stunned.

Not about to let that opportunity go to waste, she jumped on his back, grabbed his hair and banged his head against the ground a second time. A deep-throated groan followed by silence told her that he was out for the count.

Strong hands lifted her from her kneeling position. "Good going, tiger." Chap helped her stand. "You don't give up, do you?"

No, it wasn't in her to give up. Her hands ached abominably, as did her arms, but she wasn't complaining. She and Chap had taken on Lawson's men. Now it was time to take on the man himself.

* * *

Chap wanted nothing more than to get back to check on Dinkum, but he couldn't let Lawson get away. Hailey would never be truly safe until the man was behind bars. Or dead.

Before he let her inside, Chap checked every room but found no sign of his prey. Had Lawson run, like the coward he was?

No. Lawson wasn't one to give up his empire. So where was he?

"What now?" she asked.

Could Lawson have a safe room in the house? In his work for S&J, Chap had encountered several wealthy people who had had such rooms installed in their homes.

The more he thought about it, the more the idea intrigued him. He did another check of the house.

"Did Lawson ever mention any kind of safe room?" he asked.

Hailey looked thoughtful. "No. But sometimes he'd disappear for a while and then reappear like he just popped out of nowhere. Do you think there's a secret room in the house?"

"I think it's possible." They walked around the perimeter of the house, and he saw what he'd failed to notice before. The outside of the house didn't match the interior footprint.

"Look," he said, pointing to what he thought

was the kitchen. Only it appeared significantly larger than what he knew the room to be. "Isn't that the kitchen?"

"Yes, but it looks bigger out here."

They went back inside. Carefully, they went over every inch of what looked to be the exterior wall of the kitchen.

"Chap, I found something."

He turned in time to see Hailey press her palm against a panel. "No!"

At that moment, Lawson jumped out and snagged an arm around her neck. "You don't give up, do you?" Lawson lifted her off the ground, holding a lethal-looking knife to her throat.

It was a balisong. The butterfly knife was a deadly piece of steel that made the knife Klaverly had used look like a kitchen paring tool. With a dramatic flourish, Lawson flicked the weapon open and closed. He repeated the move then seated the blade.

"Like it?" he asked.

Chap rolled his lips in contempt. "It's a show-off. Like you."

Lawson's nostrils flared while his lips tightened at the corners. "You're mighty free with the insults. Especially considering I have Hailey in my hands." He slid the knife across her throat, nicking the skin slightly. Beads of blood stood in stark contrast to the pale skin of her neck.

Each drop fueled Chap's anger. "How do you look at yourself in the mirror?"

Lawson only laughed. "I've got no problem looking in the mirror, and I like what I see just fine."

"I hope you're not paying a lot for your health insurance, because you're losing money on the eyesight coverage."

"Funny man. Maybe you can take your act on the road… Never mind. You'll be dead." He nicked Hailey's throat again.

Though Hailey hadn't made a sound, Chap could see the terror in her eyes.

Chap recalled the one and only bullfight he'd ever attended. It hadn't been his idea, but a few of his teammates had wanted to see a genuine bullfight when in Spain for training with the Spanish special forces. The matador toyed with the bull, wearing him down before coming in for the kill.

Death came as a relief, both to the bull, already weakened by blood loss and exertion, and to Chap, knowing that the animal had finally been released from its suffering. The gleam of victory in Lawson's gaze was much the same as the look on the matador's eyes.

A contemptible victory that, for Chap and his teammates, held no purpose and no honor.

Just as there was no honor in what Lawson planned. He, like others of his kind, practiced cruelty for its own sake.

"You win," Chap said. "That's what you wanted, isn't it? Winning."

"Winning is everything. It's money. It's success. It's power." Lawson's eyes took on a glassy sheen as he stared at Chap speculatively. "You've got it bad for her, don't you?"

"I'm just being practical. Let her go. She won't say anything, and you don't have to worry about another body to dispose of." Chap was spouting nonsense, and he knew it. All he wanted was to keep Lawson's attention on him and off Hailey.

"I appreciate your concern, but I can handle it." Lawson skimmed the fingers of his free hand down the lapel of his designer suit as though to say he was untouchable. So caught up was he in his posturing that he didn't realize he'd released Hailey.

With that, Chap charged. It had always been going to come to this, from the moment Hailey had told him about Lawson.

Chap pulled her toward him and put her behind him.

Lawson slashed out with the knife and sliced

Chap's cheek. The men fought like two bull moose grappling for control. Blood, the sickly sweet smell of it, filled his nostrils, dribbled down his chin to his neck.

He ignored it and kept fighting.

In the right position at last, Chap dug the knuckles of his index fingers into both sides of Lawson's head until the man passed out. At the right angle and with enough strength, you could kill an opponent. Chap admitted that he was tempted.

But he didn't.

Hailey ran to him and wrapped her arms around him. "It's over." She placed her head on his chest, her soft weight melting into him.

Unable to help himself, he pressed his chin to the top of her head. Strands of her hair caught in the stubble of his beard. He'd almost lost her. Just as he'd lost Lori. He refused to be that vulnerable. Not again.

She was there, in his arms, but he was already missing her.

"It's over," he agreed.

Regret came with his next breath. What he didn't tell her was that it was over for them as well.

SIXTEEN

The last two weeks had been spent visiting Dinkum in the hospital. Characteristically, the foreman refused to be fussed over.

Hailey kissed Dinkum's cheek on her last visit. He pretended to brush it off, but she could tell that he was pleased.

"Don't you two have anything better to do than bother me when I'm supposed to be resting?" he grumbled. "You oughta be making sure that skunk Lawson never sees the light of day again."

"We're taking care of it," Chap assured his friend.

In between visits to the hospital, they'd spent their time giving statements to various authorities, including US attorneys of both Colorado and Wyoming. Because they had timed their visits individually so as to not tire Dinkum, they hadn't really seen each other one-on-one for the past two weeks. Until now.

Hailey had told her story so many times that she could repeat it in her sleep, but she didn't take any of the proceedings lightly. Putting away Lawson, his men, and all the law enforcement officers in his employ was important work. A couple of officers had flipped on him in return for reduced sentences. Reporters had dogged her steps until they had finally grown tired of her "no comment."

At last, the furor had died down.

"He won't be seeing the outside of a cell for the rest of his life," Shannon Zuniga told Chap and Hailey at the conclusion of their making a statement in Denver. Though Shannon didn't have to be there, she'd come to offer support.

Over the course of giving statements, Hailey had met several of Chap's friends and found them as committed to doing the right thing as he was.

"Thanks," Chap said. "I know you didn't have to be here, but we appreciate it."

"You've been wonderful." Hailey liked Shannon. She managed motherhood, work and running a farm with a combination of humor, patience and grace.

"It's us who should be thanking you," Shannon told Hailey. "Because of you, we'll be able to put away Lawson for life, something a lot of us have wanted to do for years."

"It was my pleasure."

Other things seemed to have fallen into place. During one trip to Colorado, they'd picked up her car so she'd have more independence.

On the way back to Wyoming, Hailey frowned, though she was careful to keep it from Chap. Now that Lawson and his people had been put away, she could look forward to a future with Chap.

Despite having to work together to get Lawson sentenced and the time spent visiting Dinkum, she noticed that Chap had been slowly pulling away from her. She did her best to convince herself that it was only a letdown from the danger they'd faced, but it felt like he'd taken a step back. A giant step.

They had each brought something to the other, something that had changed them both. She wasn't the same woman who'd stowed away in the back seat of his truck, and he was no longer the closed-off man who had rescued her. They complemented each other in the best way possible.

She had accepted Lawson's proposal with dreams of family and happily-ever-after. She hadn't found them with him, but she had found that and so much more with Chap.

"I like your friends."

"They're great," Chap agreed.

"I hope we can see them again."

"Mmm," was his non-committal reply. "They're pretty busy."

Something was off in his tone. She didn't comment on it but couldn't help a niggle of worry.

At the ranch, she set about making dinner preparations. The men had been patient with her repeated absences, but she knew they were eager for things to get back to normal.

Chap had closeted himself in his office and hadn't joined the others for the noon meal.

"Hi," she said when he made his way into the kitchen as she was cleaning up.

"We missed you at dinner."

"I was busy." The words were okay, but something was off in the tone.

"Is something wrong?" she asked when he didn't add anything more.

"Nothing's wrong. I'm just glad that whole ordeal with Lawson is over. For your sake." He averted his gaze. "I guess you'll be wanting to get back to your old life now."

She didn't respond immediately. Her old life? What was he saying?

"You won't have any trouble. You're safe now."

Safe. One of the most beautiful words in the English language.

"I can never repay you for what you did for me," she said carefully.

"You don't owe me anything. You are an amazing woman, Hailey. I hope you get everything you want in life."

You're what I want.

"Are you going to go back to your catering business?"

What was he telling her?

"I thought I had a job cooking for the men."

"You did, and you did a great job of it. But you'll be wanting to get back to your regular life now."

"What about us?" There. She'd said it. Aloud.

"You're grateful. That's all."

Hurt by the coolness of his tone, she looked at him inquiringly. "I'm grateful to you, yes, but that's not what I'm talking about."

He lifted a brow. "What *are* you talking about?"

She hesitated. How did she tell him that she loved him? Especially when his voice bordered on impatient.

"Feelings," she said at last around the breath that wanted to back up in her lungs. "I have feelings for you."

She prayed he would return the words, but he remained silent. When it became clear that he wasn't going to say anything, she plunged ahead. "I care about you. A lot."

"I care about you, too." He skimmed a hand down her cheek. His touch caused a spark— part pain, part pleasure—to spear her heart.

With that bit of encouragement, she captured his hand and brought it to her lips.

He pulled his hand away then sliced it through the air in a hard chop. "Leave it. Please. Just leave it."

The anguish in his voice tore at her heart, but she couldn't leave it there. "Are you so afraid to talk about what you feel for me?"

"You were in trouble, and I helped you out. End of story."

When he assumed another vow of silence, she decided she'd have to take the lead. "I love you, Chap."

A dismayed expression crossed his face and nearly sent her crumpling to the floor. Somehow, she stayed on her feet.

It was then that she knew with thudding certainty that he was telling her goodbye. She bit down on her lip, hoping if she focused on the pain that she wouldn't give way to the tears that were threatening.

"It wouldn't work," he said in case she hadn't gotten the message.

"If that's how you want it."

"That's how I want it." But the pain in his voice said differently.

She couldn't call him on it, though. The warning in his eyes told her to back off, and that's what she did.

Hope for a future with him had tentatively bloomed within her, but, at his words, it died. Not a slow, lingering death, but a fast punch to the heart, making it so that she couldn't breathe. She wanted to believe that she hadn't heard what he'd said, but he only looked at her with such infinite sadness that she knew she'd heard correctly.

A current of feelings did laps around her heart at the same time the breath caught in her throat.

"Goodbye, Hailey."

"We had something good," she whispered as he walked away. "Something really good. If only you could have believed."

He paused. Had her words reached him?

But no. He only continued walking away.

From what they could have had together.

From love.

From her.

Chap had taken refuge in his office later that afternoon. He couldn't get the picture of Hailey's stricken face out of his mind. When he'd left her, her eyes were the saddest he'd ever seen. Regret, compounded with a large dose of guilt, came with his next breath. The whole thing left him feeling angry. He had nothing to feel sorry for, nothing to feel guilty for. He'd done what was best. For both of them.

Eventually, Hailey would see that. He had nothing to give her. He'd seen things so horrific that the images would be with him forever. What kind of start was that for a relationship?

Still, he couldn't get over the certainty that he'd walked away from the best thing in his life, something he'd miss forever.

Hailey would go on with her life, and he'd do the same. Too bad that that life didn't include her.

He had other things in his life, didn't he? The ranch. His work at S&J. Friends. If he hadn't driven all of them away, that is. That was full enough for any man, wasn't it?

Of course it was, but a spurt of self-honesty reared its head again, causing him to question the path he'd set for himself. Hailey filled those places inside him that he wanted to keep empty. At least, he thought he had. Now, he didn't know.

It didn't improve his temper any when Dinkum pushed his way into the office. The foreman had returned home yesterday, and despite orders to take it easy, had insisted upon being up and doing a few chores.

Now he saw fit to poke his nose in where it didn't belong. "You're acting like a bear who got his head caught in a beehive and can't get it out."

"And you're acting like someone who doesn't know when to mind his own business."

Dinkum refused to back down. "I'd mind my own business if I didn't think you loved Hailey the same as she loves you. That girl loves you with all her heart, but you're too bull-headed to see it." He looked at Chap with an impatience that bordered on disgust.

"You're out of line," Chap said evenly.

"Friends oughta be able to tell each other the truth. And the truth is that you're running scared. You're scared you're gonna lose Hailey like you did Lori."

"I almost did lose her," Chap said, the last word ending on a growl. Remembered terror surged through him as he thought of Hailey with Lawson's knife at her throat. How was he supposed to forget that?

"But you didn't. She's alive and well and deserves better. If I was a few years younger, I'd make a play for her myself." Dinkum fixed him with a hard gaze, his lips thinning in anger. "Tell me you don't love her and I'll leave you be."

At Chap's silence, his friend said, "That's what I thought."

"Go away."

"Have it your way." Dinkum took himself off but not without one last parting shot. "Maybe you should ask yourself what the future's gonna look like without Hailey in it."

He ought to fire Dinkum, Chap told himself. Fire him and hire a foreman who knew his place. Even as the thought formed, he rejected it. The ranch couldn't get along without Dinkum.

Neither could he.

Sam wandered in at this moment, pushed his head against Chap's leg and looked up at him reproachfully. Or, at least, that's how it looked to Chap. He knew the big shepherd had taken a liking to Hailey, and she to him.

Sam had made a full recovery, and though Chap wanted to keep him indoors for a while, the dog insisted, as Dinkum had, on once more being part of the ranch chores.

"You come to tell me I'm making the biggest mistake of my life, too?" Chap asked.

Sam gave a plaintive sniff, as though asking where Hailey was. Then he butted his head against Chap's leg, his way of giving affection.

"I love you, too, boy," Chap said and ruffed the shepherd's neck with the back of his hand.

Guilt over how he'd treated Hailey rose in his chest, making it difficult to breathe, and try as he might, he couldn't get Dinkum's words about the future out of his head. He reminded himself that he had the ranch, his work with S&J and his friends. But a future without Hailey looked bleak; the picture conjured in his mind was one of loneliness and despair.

The realization touched a raw nerve and he felt like he'd been sucker-punched. How could he have sent her away?

Hailey gathered her few belongings, along with her battered and bruised heart. The one small bag of clothes she stowed in the trunk of her car. Her heart, she did her best to ignore.

She was glad she'd brought the car to the ranch. Otherwise, she'd be dependent upon Chap or one of his men for a ride to somewhere she could catch a bus.

The faith that had seen her through months on the street and on the run from Lawson, and through everything else life had thrown her way, would get her through this. She just had to hold on.

Hold on and trust the Lord.

Before she could leave, she had to pay one last visit to the horses.

In the barn, familiar smells wrapped their

way around her. Fresh hay and feed, the smell of the horses themselves.

Hailey would never forget them.

Tears pricked her eyes, but she refused to cry. Why should she? She and Chap didn't really know each other. Sure, they had spent time together, but most of it had been running from bad guys. She'd shared things with him, things she didn't talk about with others, and he'd done the same, but none of that made a relationship.

Could she get her catering company up and going after all this time? A few weeks away didn't seem like much, but people who needed an event catered tended to be impatient. If they couldn't get hold of her, they'd move on to someone else.

If she had to start from scratch again, she'd do it. She needed the work, not just to earn a living but for the doing. If she was doing, she wouldn't be thinking. Or feeling.

The thought took her back to that morning when Chap had told her about the threatening text message. She'd resolved then to keep working, to keep doing.

Some things hadn't changed.

Whether she started her company back up or found work elsewhere, she needed a job. Her meager savings wouldn't last more than a month. If that.

Maybe she'd ask Chap for a reference. The idea caused a mirthless smile to press her lips together. She'd get through it. Get over it. That's what she'd done in the past. That's what she'd do now.

She thought of Lawson and how she'd once believed she'd loved him. What a naïve fool she'd been. She'd been so eager for love, for family, that she hadn't seen him for what he was.

Her feelings for Lawson, when she'd believed him to be the man he'd claimed, didn't compare to her feelings for Chap. He was more. In every way. Those months with Lawson had been an aberration, something she deeply regretted. What she felt for Chap was the real thing, a love too strong to be denied, too precious to be forgotten. When she was with him, the sun shone brighter, the sky beamed bluer, the air was crisper. He filled the empty spaces in her heart and made her want to give. More. Not just to him, but to others. To the world.

Another of those mirthless smiles crossed her lips. So much for trying to convince herself that there'd been nothing between them. Whether he wanted to admit it or not, she had changed him. She had seen it in the way he'd gazed at her, warmth lighting his eyes and a quick smile curving his lips. And so, she grieved. Not just for herself, but for him.

But he didn't want her. She'd all but begged him to love her as she loved him, but he wasn't having it. Was it his feelings for Lori that stood in his way? Did he look at her—Hailey—and find her wanting?

In the end, it didn't make a difference.

A hard knot settled in her chest, balled tight, refused to uncoil. Bitter tears threatened to spill over, but she didn't give in to them. If she let them have their way, she feared she would never stop crying. A hollow ache pulsed in her heart, one of emptiness.

A cook was no stranger to pain. Especially a cook for large groups. The inevitable burns. The strained muscles from lifting huge pans of pasta or stew.

Heart pain was no different. If she told herself that often enough, she might start believing it. The enormity of this pain, though, was staggering. It felt like a giant paper cut had lacerated her chest, ripping through flesh and muscle to reach her heart.

Hailey accepted that whatever had been between them was over.

When she started outside, she saw Chap making his way toward her. They both stopped.

Stared. The Wyoming wind whipped at them with merciless persistence.

"Let's get you out of the wind," he said and led her back inside the barn. "I thought you were leaving."

"I wanted to say goodbye to the horses. I'll get out of your way now." That was a low blow, but she was feeling raw after he'd sent her away.

"I guess I deserved that."

She didn't try to talk him out of it.

"I was wrong," he said. "I messed up. Bigtime. But I was running scared."

"You? The great Michael Chapman scared? You aren't afraid of anything." She didn't bother to keep the sarcasm from her voice.

"I'm afraid of what you make me feel. I haven't felt anything since Lori died. And then you come into my life and turn it inside out."

"I'm not Lori," she pointed out.

"I was afraid I'd lose you like I lost her."

"Why tell me this now?" Hope—hadn't she thought it had died?—stirred within her.

"Because I can't live without you."

"But maybe I can live without you." She didn't want to. She wanted a home and family with him, but she accepted that she was strong enough to make a life on her own.

"I was a fool."

"I won't argue with you there." Though her

voice had gentled, she drilled a finger into his chest.

"I want you to stay. Stay on the ranch with me."

Hailey lifted a brow. "As your cook?"

"As my wife."

"It depends."

"On what?"

"If you've decided to stop being a fool."

"I'll do my best." There, in the barn, with the sweet smell of hay and the occasional snort from the horses, he kissed her. A quiet, warm kiss that felt like a promise for today and for all the days after.

"That's all I ask," she murmured.

"I love you."

She stood on tiptoe to brush a kiss across his lips. "And I love you." She pulled back to give him a considering look. "Of course, you could have said it sooner. A lot sooner. But I'm inclined to forgive you."

"Oh, you are, are you?" He kissed her once more.

"Yes," she said once she got her breath back. "Don't you know that I love you with all my heart and always will?"

"I'm beginning to figure that out."

* * * * *

Dear Reader,

Thank you for joining me once more on a journey in finding strength, faith, and love. Hailey and Chap were tested in ways they'd never thought possible, but they didn't give up.

Haven't most of us been tested, sometimes to the point where we want to throw up our hands in defeat? I know I have. I was (and am) tested with recurring bouts of chemical depression. I was tested when I watched my beloved sister die, knowing there was nothing I could do to spare her pain or to save her life.

How have you been tested? Have you had a child pull away from you? Have you or a family member suffered a devastating illness? Have you wondered if you can make a mortgage payment because you lost your job?

Being tested is part of this mortal existence as we work to find our way back to the Lord. What keeps me, and, I hope, you going is the sure knowledge that He is on our side. He will not leave us comfortless. He weeps with us when we are overwhelmed with despair, and He cheers us on when we get up to try again.

He is there.

With faith in the Lord and His continued goodness,
Jane

Get 3 FREE REWARDS!

We'll send you 2 FREE Books plus a FREE Mystery Gift.

FREE
Value Over
$20

Both the **Mystery Library** and **Essential Suspense** series feature compelling novels filled with gripping mysteries, edge-of-your-seat thrillers and heart-stopping romantic suspense stories.